IAN LIVI

FIGHTING FANTASY

Fighting Fantasy: **new Wizard editions**

1. The Warlock of Firetop Mountain
2. The Citadel of Chaos
3. Deathtrap Dungeon
4. Stormslayer
5. Creature of Havoc
6. City of Thieves

Also available in the original Wizard editions

6. Crypt of the Sorcerer
7. House of Hell
8. Forest of Doom
9. Sorcery! 1: The Shamutanti Hills
10. Caverns of the Snow Witch
11. Sorcery! 2: Kharé – Cityport of Traps
12. Trial of Champions
13. Sorcery! 3: The Seven Serpents
14. Armies of Death
15. Sorcery! 4: The Crown of Kings
16. Return to Firetop Mountain
17. Island of the Lizard King
18. Appointment with F.E.A.R.
19. Temple of Terror
20. Legend of Zagor
21. Eye of the Dragon
22. Starship Traveller
23. Freeway Fighter
24. Talisman of Death
25. Sword of the Samurai
26. Bloodbones
27. Curse of the Mummy
28. Spellbreaker
29. Howl of the Werewolf

IAN LIVINGSTONE

CITY OF THIEVES

Illustrated by Iain McCaig

Wizard Books

For Lucy

Published in the UK in 2010 by Wizard Books,
an imprint of Icon Books Ltd., Omnibus Business Centre
39–41 North Road, London N7 9DP
email: info@iconbooks.co.uk
www.iconbooks.co.uk/wizard

First published by the Penguin Group in 1983
Previously published by Wizard Books in 2003

Sold in the UK, Europe, South Africa and Asia
by Faber & Faber Ltd., Bloomsbury House
74–77 Great Russell Street, London WC1B 3DA or their agents

Distributed in the UK, Europe, South Africa and Asia
by TBS Ltd., TBS Distribution Centre, Colchester Road,
Frating Green, Colchester CO7 7DW

Published in Australia in 2010 by Allen & Unwin Pty. Ltd.,
PO Box 8500, 83 Alexander Street, Crows Nest, NSW 2065

Distributed in Canada by Penguin Books Canada,
90 Eglington Avenue East, Suite 700, Toronto,
Ontario M4P 2Y3

ISBN: 978-1-84831-113-8

Printed and bound in the UK by
Clays of Bungay

CONTENTS

HOW WILL YOU START YOUR ADVENTURE?

The book you hold in your hands is a gateway to another world – a world of dark magic, terrifying monsters, brooding castles, treacherous dungeons and untold danger, where a noble few defend against the myriad schemes of the forces of evil. Welcome to the world of **Fighting Fantasy**!

You are about to embark upon a thrilling fantasy adventure in which **YOU** are the hero! **YOU** decide which route to take, which dangers to risk and which creatures to fight. But be warned – it will also be **YOU** who has to live or die by the consequences of your actions.

Take heed, for success is by no means certain, and you may well fail in your mission on your first attempt. But have no fear, for with experience, skill and luck, each new attempt should bring you a step closer to your ultimate goal.

Prepare yourself, for when you turn the page you will enter an exciting, perilous **Fighting Fantasy** adventure where every choice is yours to make, an adventure in which **YOU ARE THE HERO!**

How would you like to begin your adventure?

If you are new to Fighting Fantasy ...
You probably want to start playing straightaway. Just turn over to the next page and start reading. You may not get very far first time but you'll get the hang of how Fighting Fantasy gamebooks work.

If you have played Fighting Fantasy before ...
You'll realise that to have any chance of success, you will need to discover your hero's attributes. You can create your own character by following the instructions on pages 201–202, or, to get going quickly, you may choose one of the existing Fighting Fantasy adventurers described on pages 198–200. Don't forget to enter your character's details on the Adventure Sheet which appears on pages 208–209.

Game Rules
It's a good idea to read through the rules which appear on pages 201–207 before you start. But as long as you have a character on your Adventure Sheet, you can get going without reading the Rules – just refer to them as you need to.

BACKGROUND

You are an adventurer in a world of monsters and magic, living by quickness of wit and skill of sword. You earn your gold as a hired warrior, usually in the employ of rich nobles and barons on missions too dangerous or difficult for their own men. Slaying monsters and fearsome beasts in pursuit of some fabled treasure comes as second nature to you. Being an experienced and highly trained swordsman, you allow nothing to stand in your way on your quests. Your success on a mission is always assured and your reputation has spread throughout the lands. Whenever you enter a village or town, the news of your arrival spreads through the citizens like wild-fire, as few of them have ever met a dragon-slayer before.

One evening, after a long walk through the outlands, you arrive at Silverton, which lies at the crossroads of the main trading routes in these parts. Great wooden wagons hauled by teams of oxen are often seen rumbling slowly through the town laden with herbs, spices, silks, metalware and exotic foods from far-off lands.

Over the years Silverton has prospered as a result of the rich merchants and traders stopping there *en route* to distant markets. Its wealth is quite apparent, with ornate buildings and richly dressed people aplenty. But as you enter the town gates, something strikes you as being not quite right. The people look nervous and on edge. Then you notice that all the windows on the buildings have great iron grills bolted over them and the doors have been strengthened too. Although you prefer your own company to that of others, you decide to stay in Silverton for the night to find out who or what is troubling the people.

As you walk down the main street, a single note from a bell rings out from a tall tower ahead. Then a man shouts, almost desperately, 'Nightfall! Nightfall! Everybody indoors!' You see people scurrying around with anxious faces, and looking surprised when they see you. Across the street you see tavern with the words 'The Old Toad' painted on its sign-board. As you enter the tavern, a whisper runs through the locals as they recognize you – some put down their mugs and stare. You are somewhat surprised that none come over to you to hear tales of adventure. Walking over to the counter you ask the old innkeeper for a room and a hot tub, but he ignores you and shuffles over to the great oak door, pushing six large iron bolts into place. Only then does he turn to you and say quietly, 'That will be five copper pieces for the room and one more for the tub, in advance if you please.' You reach into a leather pouch on your belt and toss the coins on the counter. He hands you an iron key, but at that very moment there is a loud knocking at the door followed by a voice shouting, 'Open up! Open up! This is Owen Carralif.' The old innkeeper shuffles over to the oak door again and slides open the bolts. Then a fat and balding man dressed in rich scarlet robes bursts into the tavern, looking around frantically. He sees you and walks quickly in your direction, huffing and puffing. He is a man certainly not used to haste – you notice great beads of sweat on his forehead in the pale candlelight of the room. As he nears you, he calls out urgently, 'Stranger, I must speak with you. Please sit down. It is important that I speak with you.'

When he turns to the innkeeper to snap his fingers for food and drinks, you can see that he is obviously of some standing in the town, but his face is full of anguish and sorrow. Being curious, you decide to hear what the man has to say. He pulls out a chair for you at a table, bidding you to sit down and the innkeeper bustles in with a tray laden with hot broth, roast goose and mead. The man in the scarlet robes sits opposite in silence, watching you as you feast as though examining you for some purpose of his own. Finally, as you push your plate away, the man leans forward and says, in a low but anxious voice, 'Stranger, I know of you and seek your aid. My name is Owen Carralif and I am the mayor of Silverton. We are in great trouble and danger. We are living under a curse and it is I who must rid us of it. Ten days ago two messengers of evil rode into town on huge black stallions. Stallions with fiery red eyes! It was impossible to see the faces of the riders for they wore long black cloaks with hoods pulled over their faces. Their voices were cold and each word spoken ended with an unnerving hiss. They asked for me by name and when I came to greet them, they wanted to take my beloved daughter Mirelle to stay with their master, Zanbar Bone! No doubt that you know that he is the Night Prince. Of course I refused their demand and without another word they turned and rode slowly out of the town, heads down and shoulders hunched. I knew then that beneath the cloaks were hidden the skeletal and soulless bodies of Spirit Stalkers. Zanbar Bone always uses them as his messengers as they will complete their mission or die in the attempt – and they do not die easily. Only a silver arrow through the heart will release those evil beings from their eternal twilight existence. Who knows what it would take to kill Zanbar Bone! Anyway, that same night after the Spirit Stalkers left, our troubles began. The Night Prince was angry and determined to harm us. Six Moon Dogs came, each stronger that four men, each with razor-sharp fangs. They stalked through the town, entering homes through open windows and killing the poor people inside.

In the morning we counted twenty-three dead. So we barred our windows and bolted our doors, yet each night the Moon Dogs return and we are unable to sleep for fear that they might find a way into our homes. Some people are now talking of sending Mirelle to Zanbar Bone. Those whimpering traitors, I should have them flogged! But what good would that do? There is but one hope and that rests with you, stranger. There is a man called Nicodemus who, for reasons I'll never understand, lives in Port Blacksand.

The place is commonly called the City of Thieves as it is the home of every pirate, brigand, assassin, thief and evil-doer for hundreds of miles around. I think he lives there just to get some peace from the likes of us. He is a wise old wizard and is unlikely to come to much harm even in Port Blacksand, for his magical powers are great. He alone is capable of defeating Zanbar Bone. He used to be a friend of mine many years ago. We need him and I beg you to bring him to us – none here dares enter Port Blacksand. You will be well rewarded if you help us stranger. Take these 30 Gold Pieces for your journey, and take this sword to use and keep.'

As Owen Carralif rises, he pulls back his scarlet robe, revealing the finest broadsword you have ever seen. He hands it to you and, touching the edge of the blade, you are surprised to see a droplet of blood fall from your finger. You then examine the marvellously ornate gilded serpents twining round the hilt. You have never wanted anything so badly in your life before. You stand up and hold out your right arm to Owen. He shakes it eagerly, saying, 'You must set off at the first light of dawn – the Moon Dogs will be gone by then. I shall be forced to stay the night here also, so let's drink to our destiny and may the gods be with us.'

For the next hour Owen talks about your coming journey, explaining in detail how to reach Port Blacksand. Later you gather up your backpack and furs and climb the wooden stairs to your room. You sleep uneasily despite the security afforded by your new broadsword as you are more than once woken by the sniffing, scratching and howling of the roaming Moon Dogs outside. By dawn, you are already awake and dressed, and determined to reach Port Blacksand quickly to find this man Nicodemus. As you leave the tavern, a black cat scurries past your feet and you almost trip; a bad omen perhaps?

Now turn over.

1

The walk to Port Blacksand takes you west some fifty miles across plains and over hills; fortunately without any harmful encounters. Eventually you reach the coast and see the high city wall surrounding Port Blacksand and the cluster of buildings projecting into the sea like an ugly black mark. Ships lie anchored in the harbour and smoke rises gently from chimneys. It looks peaceful enough and it is only when the wind changes that you smell the decay in the breeze to remind you of the evil nature of this notorious place. Following the dusty road north along the coast to the city gates, you begin to notice fearful warnings – skulls on wooden spikes, starving men in iron cages suspended from the city wall and black flags everywhere. As you approach the main gate a chill runs down your spine and you instinctively grip the hilt of your broadsword for reassurance. At the gate you are confronted by a tall guard wearing a black chainmail coat and iron helmet. He steps forward, barring the way with his pike, saying, 'Who would enter Port Blacksand uninvited? State the nature of your business or go back the way you came.' Will you:

Tell him you wish to be taken to Nicodemus?	Turn to **202**
Tell him you wish to sell some stolen booty?	Turn to **33**
Attack him quickly with your sword?	Turn to **49**

2

You remove the bracelet from your wrist and toss it at the oncoming monster. It lands on its armour-like shell and sticks to it like glue. You then watch as the bracelet starts to burn its way through the shell into the body of the Giant Centipede. Smoke rises from the neat round hole and as the bracelet burns deeper you can see from the frantic movements of the Centipede that it is in its death throes. Finally it is still and you manage to squeeze yourself between its body and the roof of the tunnel. You walk further down the tunnel, which ends at an iron grill through which the sewage runs. If you wish to remove the grill, turn to **377**. If you wish to walk back to the entrance hole, turn to **174**.

3

The man stops playing and tells you that he can bring you good fortune. For the sum of 3 Gold Pieces he will sing you a song that will bring you luck. If you wish to pay the musician, turn to **37**. If you do not believe him, you may walk to the next stall (turn to **398**).

4

You hear a bell ring on the other side of the door and a few minutes later the door is opened by a thin, pale-skinned man with dark, hollow eyes, who is wearing a servant's uniform. In a cold, hissing voice he says, 'Yes?' If you wish to tell him you are a lost traveller, turn to **339**. If you wish to attack him with your sword, turn to **35**.

5

Drawing your sword you leap over the counter to attack the MAN-ORC, who swiftly grabs his hand-axe. You soon realize that the Man-Orc has used his weapon before.

MAN-ORC	SKILL 8	STAMINA 5

If you win, turn to **371**.

6

Her tone becomes unpleasant and she tells you to get out of her house because there are certainly no rags in it, nor any other kind of jumble for that matter. If you wish to obey her, leave the house and head further north along Stable Street, turn to **333**. If you wish to go through the curtains and see who is being so rude to you, turn to **88**.

7

You tiptoe quietly out of the room and close the door. In the corridor you open the pouch and find six black pearls. Add 2 LUCK points. If you have not already done so, you may open the other door (turn to **232**), or leave the ship to continue your search of Port Blacksand by walking north up Harbour Street (turn to **78**).

8

The creature pins the golden brooch to your leather tunic and you pay the price demanded. You have bought a lucky charm – add 2 LUCK points to your total. Pleased with your purchase you leave the house and head north (turn to **334**).

9

You step back from the vile body of Zanbar Bone, waiting for him to decay. However, you have chosen wrongly! He pulls the arrow from his chest and rubs the compound from his eyes. He sees you and laughs. You are mesmerized by his power and are unable to move. He walks up to you and touches your face with his skeletal fingers. Your life is draining quickly away and you will soon begin your undead existence as a servant of Zanbar Bone.

10

The GUARD is really annoyed and charges at you with his pike.

CITY GUARD SKILL 8 STAMINA 7

If you win and the fight lasts six Attack Rounds or less, turn to **212**. If the fight lasts longer than six Attack Rounds, turn to **130**.

11

The Trolls see what you are doing and run towards the tree. You are forced to leave your shield behind. Lose 1 SKILL point. After climbing quickly up the tree you realize that you must jump a distance of two metres between the branch and the top of the wall. If you are wearing a chainmail coat you will have to take it off in order to jump safely across to the wall (lose 2 SKILL points). Below, you see the two Trolls running round the tree waving their swords at you. There is no alternative but to jump (turn to **358**).

12

After a few minutes you hear footsteps coming down the corridor. The door opens and a man walks into the room wearing nothing but a towel round his fat stomach. You watch as he drops the towel and lowers himself gently into the tub with a loud sigh. If you wish to surprise him by drawing your sword and uttering a loud 'Ahem!', turn to **176**. If you would rather creep out of the room back into the corridor while he submerges himself, turn to **383**.

13

Inspecting the scorpion you see that it is a brooch. You decide to pin it to your leather tunic. The brooch has magic healing properties: after any battle, the brooch will immediately restore 1 STAMINA point to your total.

What will you do next? You may, if you have not already done so, pick up the golden scorpion (turn to **273**). If you would rather ignore it, you may either climb the stairs (turn to **80**), or leave the house and head north (turn to **334**).

14

As soon as you pluck one of the flowers you hear the noise of rustling leaves. Three of the animal-shaped hedges have uprooted themselves and are closing in on you. Do you have a Ring of Fire? If you have, turn to **237**. If not, turn to **191**.

15

You leap over the snakes and run for the door. *Test your Luck*. If you are Lucky, you reach the door safely (turn to **75**). If you are Unlucky, one of the snakes strikes out and bites you on the leg (turn to **298**).

16

The bag holds 12 Gold Pieces. Add 1 LUCK point. You leave the house quickly before the owner discovers you are not who you say you are. You then walk further north along Stable Street (turn to **333**).

17

Walking along the narrow street you see a man wearing tattered rags sitting in the gutter. His head rests on his hands and he looks thoroughly miserable. If you wish to stop to talk to him, turn to **331**. If you would rather continue walking east, turn to **161**.

18

You take aim carefully and throw the knife at the leading vagabond. Roll two dice. If the total is the same or less than your SKILL score, the knife sinks

deep into the vagabond's chest, stopping him dead in his tracks (turn to **102**). If the total is greater than your SKILL score, the knife flies past its target and you must fight all three vagabonds with your sword (turn to **225**).

19

The darts are poison-tipped. Lose 4 STAMINA points and 1 SKILL point. If you are still alive and wish to continue picking the lock, turn to **340**. If you would rather leave the room and climb the stairs to the floor above, turn to **60**.

20

The pirate's pockets contain nothing apart from a piece of stale bread. You leave him to start a search of the wooden boxes and barrels on the ship's deck (turn to **84**).

21

Looking up, you see that the staircase goes all the way up to the top of the tower. You stop off at the first floor and walk along the landing to a door. The door opens into a large room which contains a comfortable, made-up bed. If you wish to lock the door and go to sleep for the night, turn to **288**. If you wish to explore the tower further, turn to **77**.

22

As you sit down at the table the GOBLINS stop their quarrelling and stare at you coldly. You see hatred in their brown warty faces. Suddenly they stand up and draw their swords. You must fight them one at a time.

	SKILL	STAMINA
First GOBLIN	4	5
Second GOBLIN	5	5

If you win, turn to **198**.

23

The man grabs a wooden club from behind a chair and prepares to fight you. He is strong but not a good fighter.

SILVERSMITH SKILL 4 STAMINA 8

If you win, turn to **146**.

24

There is another shop on the left side of the street. An iron grill over the window prevents you seeing what kind of shop it is. You try the handle on the door and it turns. If you want to enter the shop, turn to **336**. If you wish to continue west, without looking into the shop, turn to **196**.

25

You soon realize you are in a stable when you see a large, bare-chested man wearing a grubby white apron busy at work at an open fire. He takes a red-hot iron bar from the fire with his gloved hand and starts to hammer it into the shape of a horseshoe on his anvil. Sweat pours from his brow as he toils with the hammer. Will you:

Make conversation with the blacksmith? — Turn to **169**
Attack him with your sword? — Turn to **323**
Leave him to his labours and continue north? — Turn to **115**

26

You sheathe your sword and look round at the circle of spectators. Having witnessed your excellent swordsmanship each goes quietly back to his table, not wishing to anger you any further. The innkeeper apologizes for his unfriendliness and invites you to sit at the bar and enjoy a drink at his expense. You ask him if he knows the whereabouts of Nicodemus. The innkeeper frowns and looks at you inquiringly. Then he says, 'I don't know what you want from that wily old wizard. He keeps himself to himself and lives alone in a small hut under Singing Bridge. Keep walking north along Market Street, through the market-place, and you'll come to a bridge that crosses Catfish River and leads to the old part of the city and the harbour. Nicodemus won't talk to you and he knows enough magic to keep even the toughest away from his door.' You tell the innkeeper not to be so discourteous to strangers next time, and leave the tavern to head north (turn to **296**).

27

You enter a small candlelit room with no windows. It is empty apart from a table and two chairs. A man wearing black robes and a skullcap is standing in a corner. He smiles and asks you to sit down at the table. He sits opposite you and, after placing six white pills on top of six skulls on the table, looks up to you and says, 'One of the pills before you is deadly poisonous, the others are harmless. Swallow one of your choice. If you live, I will give you 20 Gold Pieces. If you die, I keep all your possessions.' If you wish to play this deadly game, turn to **223**. If you would rather leave this room and walk back up the alley to Candle Street, turn to **165**.

28

While you were fighting the Giant Rats, you thought you saw someone or something skulking in the shadows ahead. If you wish to continue further north along the tunnel, turn to **265**. If you would rather turn round and walk back to the entrance hole, turn to **104**.

29

You squat down on the mattress and consider what to do next. If you wish to feign illness and throw the iron pail against the bars of the cell to attract the guards' attention, turn to **143**. If you wish to inspect the cell closely in the hope of finding a secret escape route, turn to **230**.

30

Tower Street soon ends at a junction, where it meets Stable Street running north and south. You decide to go north (turn to **76**).

31

Ahead you see a wooden bridge stretching over a dirty river. Various bits of rubbish are floating down to the sea on its black surface, and you squirm at the sight of a human hand passing by. The bridge supports and columns reach high above and you see skulls, both human and non-human, tied to them. The wind makes an eerie noise as it whistles through the bridge structures, reminding you of tortured souls crying out for help. Almost hidden from view is a small flight of steps going down underneath the bridge from where you are standing. A one-legged man carrying a sack is crossing the bridge from the northern bank. If you wish to climb down the steps, turn to **329**. If you wish to wait to talk to the man, turn to **364**.

32

Before you reach the door, the Serpent Queen extends her head and bites you on the neck, causing the loss of 4 STAMINA points and 1 SKILL point. If you are still alive, you draw your sword to attack the Serpent Queen (turn to **249**).

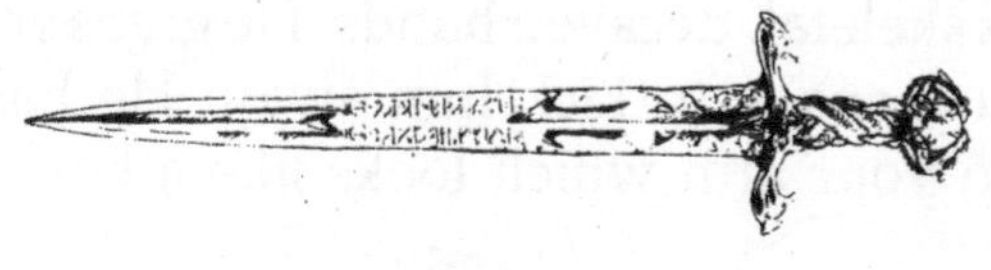

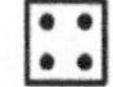 

33

You tell the guard that you wish to sell some silver chalices that you stole from a tavern in Silverton and that you will pay him a Gold Piece for his advice as to where to go for the best price. The guard looks at you suspiciously, saying, 'Let me look at these chalices in your backpack before I admit you.' Will you:

Tell him that you know the chalices are cursed and should only be examined by a mage? Turn to **381**
Try to run past the guard into the main street? Turn to **291**
Attack him quickly with your sword? Turn to **49**

34

The carriage thunders by and you see its driver urging on the four horses as though his life depended on it. As the noise of the carriage fades into the distance, you step out on to the street and continue west (turn to **171**).

35

You push the man through the doorway and run him through with your sword. Much to your surprise he is unaffected by the wound. Slowly he advances towards you, trying to touch your skin with his skeletal, decayed hands. He grabs your arm but you manage to kick him away. He has left a mark on your arm which looks like a burn, but it emits a revolting smell of putrid flesh. Lose 2 STAMINA points. Then you realize that before you stands a Spirit Stalker, one of the faithful servants of Zanbar Bone. As he advances towards you again with his arms outstretched, you try to remember what you must do. Will you:

Fire the silver arrow at him? Turn to **189**
Reflect his stare in your mirror
(if you have one)? Turn to **305**
Fire your Ring of Ice at him
(if you have one)? Turn to **382**

36

The man leans on the counter and tells you that a Ring of Invisibility costs 10 Gold Pieces, a Ring of Fire costs 8 Gold Pieces, and a Ring of Ice costs 7 Gold Pieces. If you wish to buy one of the rings, make the necessary deduction on your *Adventure Sheet*. Bidding the man farewell, you slip the ring on your finger and leave the shop to head west (turn to **196**).

37

The man strums his lyre and sings a merry song all about you and your good fortune – he does have the power to make you lucky. Add 2 LUCK points and walk on to the next stall (turn to **398**).

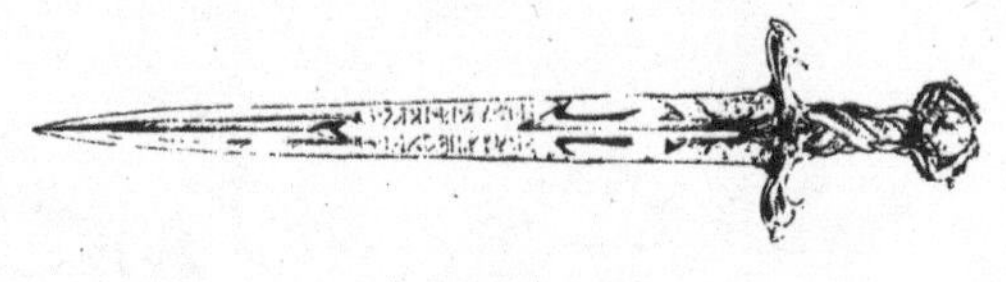

charge!

38

One of the men reaches into a pocket inside his green jacket and produces a thin silver bracelet. He gives it to you and you see the outline of an insect etched into its surface. The man explains that the insect bracelet has the power to kill even giant insects. After placing the bracelet on your wrist you leave the tavern and head north again (turn to **296**).

39

You open your backpack and pretend to search for the silver item. The Serpent Queen starts to fidget and you can see her becoming increasingly impatient. You cannot think of a good plan and start to panic. If you wish to run to the front door, turn to **32**. If you wish to draw your sword to attack the Serpent Queen, turn to **249**.

40

From the top of the wall you see that it encircles a group of brown creatures playing some kind of game with a wooden stick and a small leather ball. One of the creatures has just hit the ball and is running towards a creature from the other team who has his foot on a cloth bag. You realize that these creatures are Bays playing their favourite game, Bays' Ball. If you wish to ask to join in their game, turn to **168**. If you would rather climb back down the wall, return to the junction and head west down Harbour Street, turn to **91**.

41

The two guards holding you look at each other and then at the other guard for a decision. He nods at them and they release their grip on you. As you pay him the 15 Gold Pieces he gives you a piercing look, saying, 'If Lord Azzur finds out that you are in the city without a pass, you are as good as dead. I'd get one if I were you. And as for Nicodemus, find him yourself.' Repressing an urge to draw your sword you turn and walk into the city (turn to **74**).

42

You tell the man that you cannot pay the price he is asking. He shrugs his shoulders and says, 'Well, do you have any food?' You open your backpack and he takes all your remaining Provisions. He then starts to cast the silver arrow and you wait patiently as he makes it. Finally he presents you with it and assures you that it will be accurate in flight. You thank him for his trouble and leave his shop. Outside you set off east once again (turn to **100**).

43

You cry out in pain as the goblet changes into a burning coal in your hand. You are badly burnt. Lose 2 SKILL and 2 LUCK points. If you have not done so already you may lift goblet A (turn to **175**) or goblet B (turn to **209**). If you are not interested in the goblets, you may either walk through the archway (turn to **107**) or climb the stairs (turn to **60**).

44

Standing in a line across the street are three tall men each armed with a spiked club. You notice that each has a red star tattooed on his forehead. They are vagabonds intent on robbing you. If you have a Throwing Knife you may be able to cut one down before they reach you (turn to **18**). If you do not have a Throwing Knife you will have to fight all three with your sword (turn to **225**).

45

The glass ball shatters on impact with the cobbled street. On contact with the air the smoke turns a golden colour and begins to take the shape of a winged helmet. The helmet solidifies and rests on the street, sparkling in the sunlight. It is the most magnificent helmet you have ever seen. If you wish to place it on your head, turn to **376**. If you would rather leave it alone and set off east again, turn to **161**.

46

The blacksmith takes your money and walks over to some bales of hay in the corner. He lifts one up and underneath it you see the chainmail coat. He turns to you and says, 'You have to hide everything in this place. You can't trust anybody.' The coat fits perfectly and its workmanship is excellent. Add 2 SKILL points. You leave the stables with your new armour and continue north (turn to **115**).

47

The lightning bolt slams into your chest and knocks you to the floor. Lose 3 STAMINA points. If you are still alive you see the fat man roaring with laughter. Perhaps he is off his guard? You decide to throw your sword at him from your prone position. Roll two dice. If the number rolled is less than or equal to your SKILL score, the sword pierces the chest of the man and kills him (turn to **313**). If the number is greater than your SKILL score, the sword flies past him and clatters on to the marble floor (turn to **81**).

48

There is an iron ladder secured to the rim of a hole, descending into a tunnel below. It is dark, and a very unpleasant smell rises up from below. If you wish to climb down the ladder, turn to **321**. If you wish to replace the manhole cover and continue east, turn to **205**.

49

As you draw your sword the guard leaps to his right and attempts to ring a small bell on the wall of the guardhouse. *Test your Luck.* If you are Lucky, he misses the bell, curses, and turns to fight you with his pike (turn to **10**). If you are Unlucky, he manages to grab the bell and rings it loudly before turning to fight you with his pike (turn to **311**).

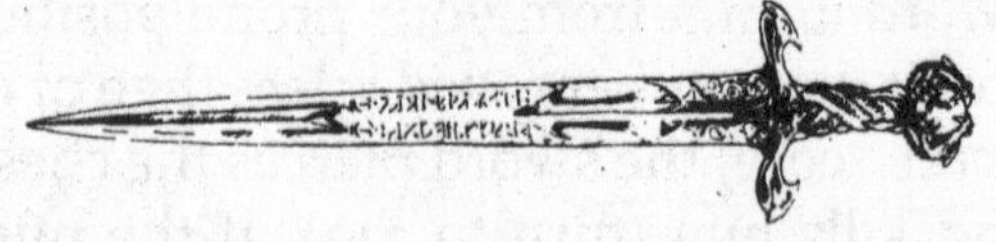

50

The stairs lead down into the ship's cargo hold. It is empty. Opposite you a corridor leads from the hold to two closed doors. You walk along the corridor and listen at the doors. From the door on your left you hear loud snoring. From the door on your right you hear nothing. If you wish to open the door on the left, turn to **271**. If you wish to open the door on the right, turn to **232**.

51

You walk over to the old man and help him to his feet. He is very grateful and offers to buy you a drink at a nearby tavern. If you wish to go for a drink, turn to **325**. If you would rather continue your quest, turn to **348**.

52

Behind the next stall is a young man selling small weapons and items of equipment. The prices of his wares are chalked up on a slate:

Throwing Knife	4 Gold Pieces
Climbing Rope	2 Gold Pieces
Butcher's Meat Hook	2 Gold Pieces
Iron Spike	1 Gold Piece
Lantern	3 Gold Pieces

If you wish to buy some or all of the items, make the necessary adjustments on your *Adventure Sheet*. You then walk north (turn to **200**).

53

The silk curtains in front of the archway are pulled aside and a strange creature steps into the room. It has a snake's head, which sits oddly atop the body of a young woman wearing a lavish gown. Its mouth opens and a forked tongue darts in and out as the Serpent Queen says, 'Don't try to fool me, I know that scoundrel Borryman never sends flowers. What silver gift have you brought me?' If you have a silver item in your backpack that you wish to give to the Serpent Queen, turn to **328**. If you have not got a silver item that you wish to give away, turn to **39**.

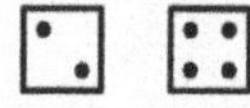

54

You search the guardhouse and find 2 Gold Pieces and a merchant's pass permitting the holder to trade in Port Blacksand. Taking your findings with you, you creep outside. The guard at the main gate does not see you and you walk into the city (turn to 74).

55

You dip the petals of the flower in the spilled blood of the dead dogs. On contact with blood the petals sparkle and make a popping noise. On the floor are 10 Gold Pieces. You pick up the gold and walk back up the alleyway to Harbour Street, where you turn left (turn to 180).

56

There are over twenty guards coming to get you and it is useless to put up a fight. They drag you off to a room at the bottom of the tower and chain you to a wall. To your horror you see the two Trolls enter the room. They take it in turns to beat you before passing a sentence of five years' solitary confinement in a dungeon cell. A few minutes later a hunchbacked jailer arrives carrying a bull-hide whip. He fixes a ball and chain to your leg before leading you downstairs to begin your jail sentence. You have failed in your mission.

57

The Dwarf jumps up off his stool, his face full of hatred. He calls out two names loudly and two huge black dogs immediately appear from under a table with long fangs protruding from their slavering mouths. Wraggins points a finger at you, shouting 'Kill the friend of Nicodemus!' and the dogs leap at you, barking wildly. You must fight them for your life, one at a time.

	SKILL	STAMINA
First WOLF DOG	7	7
Second WOLF DOG	7	5

If you win, turn to **360**.

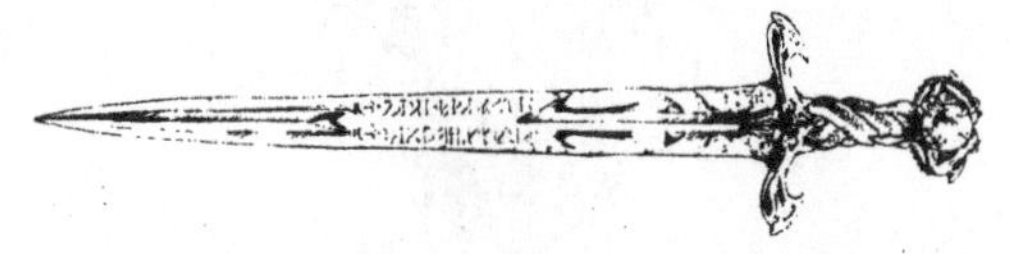

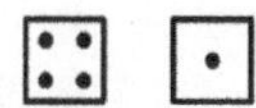

58

As the carriage thunders by, the driver lashes out at you with his whip. Lose 1 STAMINA point. You curse the driver of the carriage as it races out of view, rubbing your neck where the whip has raised a weal. You set off west again (turn to 171).

59

The Hag laughs as she watches you in the throes of your nightmare. Then from out of her clothing she pulls a dagger with a long shimmering blade. You are helpless and unable to stop her plunging the dagger into your chest. Tonight her stew-pot will contain more than rat meat. Your adventure ends here.

60

At the top of the stairs you reach a landing with two closed doors. As you are deciding which door to enter, you hear a noise from downstairs – somebody is entering the front door. Then you hear a man's voice saying, 'Off you fly, my little beauty, find the intruder.' If you wish to draw your sword in readiness, turn to **349**. If you would rather make a break for it, you may jump out of the window at the head of the landing into the street below (turn to **192**).

61

The silk curtains in front of the archway are pulled aside and a strange creature steps into the room. It has a snake's head, which sits oddly atop the body of a young woman wearing a lavish gown. You feel uncomfortable and are undecided whether or not to draw your sword. Then the snake's mouth opens and a forked tongue darts in and out as the Serpent Queen asks to see the flowers sent to her by Lord Azzur. If you have a bunch of flowers, turn to **172**. If you do not have a bunch of flowers, turn to **350**.

62

The old wooden doors open into a dingy, smoke-filled room. There are eight round tables in the centre of the room with some of the most mean and shifty-looking rogues you have ever seen sitting at them. At the back of the tavern is a long wooden bar covered with bottles and mugs. Behind the bar stands the innkeeper wearing a grubby apron. He is quite old, bald and has an ugly black scar running down his right cheek. Not all the customers are human. Will you:

Walk to the bar to talk to the innkeeper? Turn to **136**
Sit down at a table with three Dwarfs who are playing a dice game? Turn to **173**
Sit down at a table with two Goblins who are arguing? Turn to **22**
Sit down with three men who are sticking daggers quickly between their fingers on the table? Turn to **190**
Leave the tavern and walk north? Turn to **296**

63

The Elf leads you into a room lit by purple candles, which give a strange glow. You stand and stare blankly at the candles and drift off into a world of vivid dreams. While you are in this trance, the Elf takes two items and 5 Gold Pieces from your back-pack (if you have them). When you awake, you

have no recollection of the theft and leave the shop thanking the Elf for showing you his beautiful candles. Outside you head east again (turn to **280**).

64

You hear growls and loud barking coming from inside the kennel, and suddenly an enormous black wolf rushes out of the kennel straight at you. A long chain is attached to its collar and this may stop it from reaching you. *Test your Luck.* If you are Lucky, the chain pulls taut and the wolf jerks to a halt (turn to **353**). If you are Unlucky, the chain remains slack and the wolf leaps up and bites your arm. Lose 1 STAMINA point and turn to **309**.

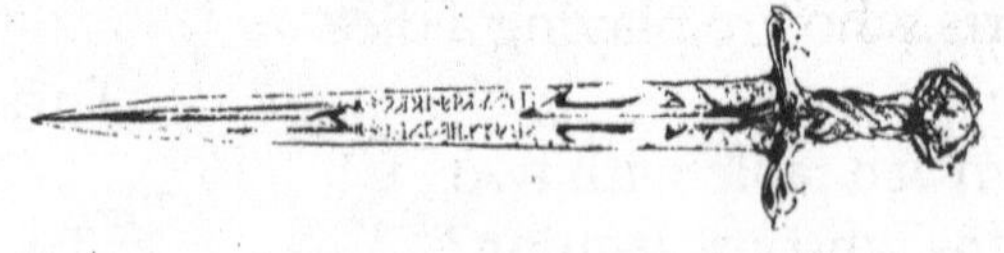

65

On the next floor there are two doors adjacent to one another on the landing. One is painted white and the other black. Suddenly a voice calls out from nowhere, saying, 'Oh foolish adventurer, why do you even consider it a remote possibility that you can defeat me, the almighty Zanbar Bone. I am following your every move, but you do not know where I am. Ha! Ha! Ha!' Will you:

Open the white door?	Turn to **319**
Open the black door?	Turn to **96**
Carry on up the stairs?	Turn to **197**

66

The Dwarf smiles and boasts that he can make a key to open any lock in Port Blacksand. He says that his special keys are priced at 10 Gold Pieces each. If you want to buy a key, make the necessary deduction on your *Adventure Sheet*. Whether or not you buy a key you leave the shop and continue west (turn to **300**).

67

The woman's voice sounds excited as she calls through the curtains, 'Oh, I wonder which kind dear has sent me flowers? Can you tell me who they are from?' If you wish to tell her a name, turn to **195**. If you wish to tell her that you do not know who they are from, turn to **79**.

68

The soup tastes absolutely disgusting. If you wish to swallow it, turn to **380**. If you wish to spit it out, turn to **262**.

69

Just as the guards are about to lead you away, you try with all your might to pull your arms from their grip. Roll two dice. If the number rolled is less than or equal to your SKILL score, you succeed – turn to **355**. If the number rolled is greater than your SKILL, you fail to release yourself, and are led away, struggling violently (turn to **151**).

70

As you reach the chest it disappears before your eyes. You hear laughter behind you and suddenly see in the mirror the hideous reflection of a black-robed skeleton with green, translucent eyes, wearing a golden crown on its skull. You spin round but it's too late. Zanbar Bone's skeletal fingers are touching your flesh and are draining your life away. You are now one of his undead servants.

71

The Ogre's room is full of clutter and discarded bits and pieces. It does not appear to have been tidied for years. Rummaging through the jumble, you find a polished wooden box with a hand made of white shell inlaid on the lid. The box is locked and you cannot find the key to open it. If you wish to smash it open with your sword, turn to **324**. If you wish to leave the house to continue north, without trying to open the box, turn to **282**.

72

As you bend down to help the injured boy, he suddenly rolls over and you see the flashing blade of a dagger before your eyes. The boy is in fact a GOBLIN thief and you must fight him for your life.

GOBLIN	SKILL 5	STAMINA 4

If you win, turn to **208**.

73

You draw your sword and stand ready to fight the Trolls. They seem pleased that you are going to give them a chance to practise their beloved sport of killing humans, and advance towards you swinging their battle-axes. Sourbelly snarls and says, 'Stand back, Fatnose – let me deal with this dog alone.' Fight them one at a time.

	SKILL	STAMINA
SOURBELLY	10	11
FATNOSE	9	10

If you win, turn to **110**. You may *Escape* after killing Sourbelly by throwing your shield at Fatnose and running off west along Mill Street. Lose 1 SKILL point and turn to **239**.

74

Through the main gates you see that the rubbish-filled streets of the port are narrow and cobbled. Old and decrepit buildings line them closely, with their upper storeys overhanging menacingly. You may:

Go west down Key Street	Turn to **95**
Head north along Market Street	Turn to **116**
Go east down Clock Street	Turn to **17**

75

Outside the rain has stopped and you set off north again (turn to **31**).

76

To your left you see a large wooden barn set back from the houses. Two horses are tied to a post outside the barn, and smoke rises from a crooked chimney on top of its low flat roof. If you wish to walk through the barn doors, turn to **25**. If you would rather continue north, turn to **115**.

77

You walk quietly back to the staircase and climb up to the second floor. Again there is a door at the end of the landing. If you wish to open the door, turn to **292**. If you wish to climb up to the third floor, turn to **310**.

78

The street runs north along the quayside for a few hundred metres before arriving at a junction. If you wish to continue north up Harbour Street, turn to **256**. If you wish to walk east along Clog Street, turn to **216**.

79

The silk curtains in front of the archway are suddenly pulled aside and a strange creature steps into the room. It has a snake's head, which sits oddly atop the body of a young woman wearing a lavish gown. Its mouth opens and a forked tongue darts in and out as the SERPENT QUEEN challenges you, saying, 'Do not lie to me, scoundrel. No doubt you are an assassin come here to kill me. But you shall die instead!' Suddenly the Serpent Queen stretches out her head and bites you on the neck. Lose 4 STAMINA points and 1 SKILL point. If you are still alive, you draw your sword to defend yourself.

SERPENT QUEEN SKILL 9 STAMINA 7

If you win, turn to **295**.

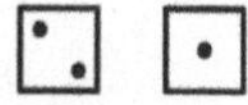

80

The stairs lead into a small room, again painted red. Sitting at a table is a strange creature with a long snout and deep red, scaly skin. From its jaw protrude rows of sharp teeth and a long pink tongue darts quickly in and out between them. The creature looks up and stares at you. Are you wearing a scorpion brooch? If you are, turn to **392**. If not, turn to **215**.

81

The man laughs even louder and mocks your attempt to kill him. You decide to leap up and make a dash for the front door, picking up your sword as you run. The man sees what you are doing and fires another lightning bolt at you. *Test your Luck*. If you are Lucky, the lightning bolt misses you, and you manage to open the door and run north up the street (turn to **304**). If you are Unlucky, the lightning bolt thuds into your back and you cry out in pain (turn to **243**).

82

Before the Hag can complete her spell, you reach into your backpack and take out the bottle containing the potion. You gulp down the liquid and feel its effects immediately. The Hag is still mouthing her vile sorcery but you cannot hear her. Safe from her evil, you draw your sword and step forward. You grab hold of her matted hair and cut a clump from her head. She writhes and kicks and spits at you. At this close range you can see fresh blood on her face –

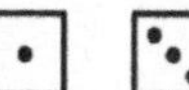

no doubt she could not wait to cook some of the rats she had killed. Despite your repulsion you are excited about having gained one of the items necessary to defeat the Night Prince. You throw the Hag into the sewer and walk back to the entrance hole (turn to **104**).

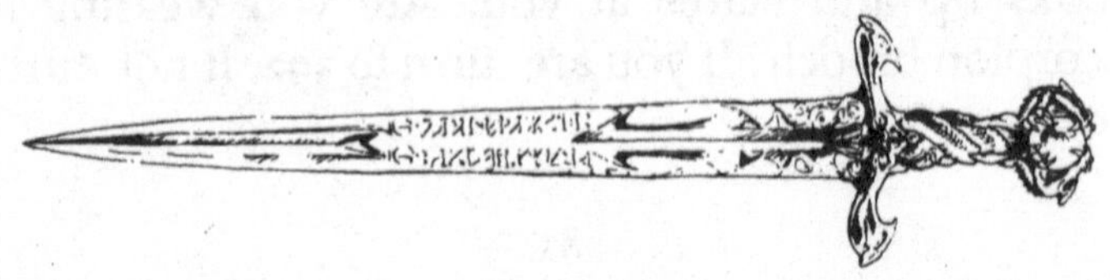

83

Fortunately, the contents of the jar are as the label reads, although the strength of the mixture is unpredictable. Roll 1 die. The number rolled is the number of STAMINA points that will be restored. If you wish to continue searching the shop, turn to **322**. If you would rather leave the shop to head north, turn to **93**.

84

The barrels all contain rotten fruit and the boxes contain manacles and leg irons. Perhaps this is a slave-trading ship. There is nothing else of interest to you on deck. If you wish to walk over to the deck cabin to climb down the stairs to the lower decks, turn to **50**. If you would rather leave the ship, walk back along the jetty, turn left and walk north up Harbour Street, turn to **78**.

85

You pay the silversmith and wait patiently while he makes a silver arrow for you. Finally he presents you with it and assures you that it will be completely accurate in flight. You thank him for his trouble and leave his shop. Outside you set off east once again (turn to **100**).

86

A leather pouch hanging round the neck of the man contains a small glass ball containing what looks like swirling smoke. Will you:

Smash the ball on the ground?	Turn to **45**
Put the ball in your backpack?	Turn to **194**
Leave the ball behind and continue east?	Turn to **161**

87

You reach the top of the ladder and peer over the handrail to survey the ship's deck. There are two large masts rising into the air from the deck. Wooden boxes, barrels and coils of rope lie all around, and one of the ship's crew stands on guard at the top of the gangplank. In the centre of the deck there is a small cabin with an open door. Through the door you see stairs leading down to the lower decks. If you wish to inspect any of the wooden boxes and barrels, you will have to deal with the pirate on guard (turn to **120**). If you wish to creep along the deck to the stairs, turn to **50**.

88

You pull back the curtains and walk into a very lavish boudoir. In it is a young woman with her back towards you. As you approach her she spins round and you are stunned to see, not the young woman's face you are expecting, but a large snake's head. It extends out from the shoulders and bites you on the neck. You are caught somewhat off-balance by the SERPENT QUEEN and suffer the loss of 4 STAMINA points and 1 SKILL point before you can draw your sword to defend yourself.

SERPENT QUEEN SKILL 9 STAMINA 7

If you win, turn to **295**. You may *Escape* after three Attack Rounds by running out of the house and north along Stable Street (turn to **333**).

89

As you slide your hand into the glove, it seems to come alive and cling tightly to your hand. Then it changes texture and becomes hot and you feel as though your hand is covered with burning tar which you are unable to shake off. Mercifully it cools down, but a thin white film remains on your hand, making it difficult to open and close. Lose 2 SKILL points. You curse and leave the house to head north (turn to **282**).

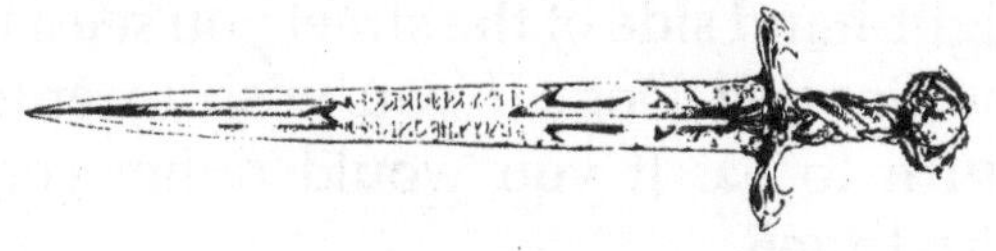

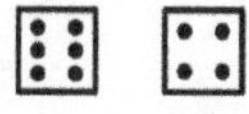

90

You swing your sword with all your strength and bring it down on the heavy chain. Much to your surprise it bounces off. Before you have time to try again, you are surrounded by four town guards who are pointing their pikes at you. Will you:

Tell them you have caught the escaped prisoner for them?	Turn to **199**
Offer them a bribe to let you and the prisoner go free?	Turn to **187**

91

You pass a beggar in the street. He is sitting in the gutter and holds an empty tin in his hand. If you wish to toss a Gold Piece into his tin, turn to **332**. If you would rather walk past him, turn to **124**.

92

You are slowly feeling your way along the bricks when your hand comes into contact with a smooth flat object. You pull it out and see that you are holding a mirror. You pack it away and walk back to the entrance hole (turn to **174**).

93

On the right-hand side of the street you see a tavern called the Spotted Dog. If you wish to enter the tavern, turn to **62**. If you would rather continue north, turn to **296**.

94

The little man smiles and says, 'Easy.' He reaches into his pocket and produces some sparkling dust which he throws up at you. As it settles on your clothes, a feeling of strength surges through your body. Add 6 STAMINA points. He then tells you that as he is feeling particularly grateful he will grant you another wish. With your strength returned you feel you can now deal with Zanbar Bone and ask the little man of his whereabouts (turn to **234**).

95

On the left side of the street you see a large iron key hanging over the doorway of a small shop. A sign in the window reads 'J. B. Wraggins, Locksmith'. If you want to enter the shop, turn to **224**. If you would rather continue walking west, turn to **300**.

96

You open the door and enter a room which is adorned with macabre objects and paintings. A black cat is sitting in front of a table covered in black cloth. Two black candles are burning on either side of a mirror on the far wall. On the table lies an open chest containing a golden skull. Will you:

Walk over to the chest? — Turn to **257**

Close the door and open the white door (if you have not done so already)? — Turn to **319**

Close the door and walk back to the staircase to climb up to the next floor? — Turn to **197**

97

You decide to take a quick look inside the kennel. Hanging on a hook is an iron key which you place in your pocket. Add 1 LUCK point and turn to **353**.

98

You uncork the bottle with your teeth and take a long gulp of the liquid. Fortunately the liquid is what the man claims it to be. Add 3 STAMINA points and 1 LUCK point. Well-refreshed, you set off east again, bidding the old man farewell (turn to **363**).

99

You are unable to explain why you are in Port Blacksand and the guards draw their swords, telling you that you are under arrest. You draw your sword and fight them one at a time.

	SKILL	STAMINA
First CITY GUARD	7	4
Second CITY GUARD	6	6

If you win, turn to **285**.

100

You soon arrive at a junction. If you wish to turn north into Tower Street, turn to **127**. If you wish to continue east into Stable Street, turn to **246**.

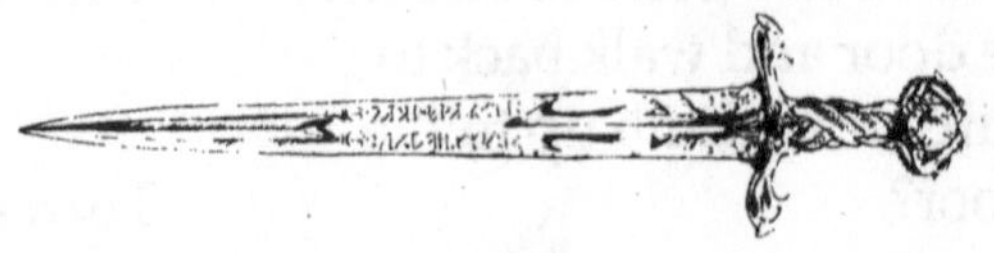

101

You enter the shop and see the Man-Orc standing behind the counter. He is smiling at your misfortune and says, 'Huh, can't even take Old Trollborn. And don't think I am going to give you your money back.' If you wish to attack the impudent Man-Orc, turn to **5**. If you would rather leave the shop and head north again, containing your anger, turn to **93**.

102

The other two vagabonds stop to aid their friend, but it is too late, as he is already dead. They seem undecided as to what to do next. After a brief conversation they pick up their dead friend and carry him off down a narrow alleyway to your right. You walk quickly north before they have time to reappear with more of their gang (turn to **372**).

103

You arrive at a four-way junction in the street. The street continuing east changes its name to Clock Street and the street running north and south is called Market Street. Looking north you see a crowd of people walking up the street cheering loudly and waving their arms in the air. You decide to follow them (turn to **148**).

104

Back at the entrance hole you may either climb up the ladder to the street in order to continue east (turn to **205**) or, if you have not done so already, you may walk south along the sewer (turn to **118**).

105

Most of the houses in the street are joined in a long terrace, but you see one on the left side that stands alone and is set back. There appears to be a large wooden kennel outside the heavy oak front door. If you wish to approach the front door, turn to **64**. If you wish to keep walking north, turn to **304**.

106

The Lantern breaks on impact with the Mummy and covers it with burning oil. Flames spread quickly along the dry bandages and the Mummy is soon consumed by fire. If you wish to inspect the open sarcophagus, turn to **163**. If you wish to leave the room immediately, turn to **231**.

107

The back room is as lavishly furnished as the front room. In the far corner you see a wooden chest bolted to the floor. It is securely locked. If you wish to try to pick the lock, turn to **128**. If you wish to leave the room and climb the stairs to the floor above, turn to **60**.

108

You lower yourself slowly to the ground. Above you the guards are waving their fists at you from the battlements. You are now outside Port Blacksand. Do you have all the necessary items required to slay the Night Prince? If you have them all and have been tattooed, turn to **201**. If you lack any of the items or have not been tattooed, turn to **299**.

109

The guards look at each other and burst out laughing. Then one says, 'Do you think we would risk letting you in Port Blacksand for the sake of 5 Gold Pieces? If Lord Azzur found out that we let you in without a pass, we would be dead men. Let's hear no more about bribes, it's the dungeon for you.' Turn to **151**.

110

Your fight attracted a group of onlookers. Some of the beggars even cheered when you cut down old Sourbelly. But one sly-looking character sloped off with the obvious intention of finding more guards. It is dangerous to stay here any longer, so you run off west along Mill Street (turn to **239**).

111

You cut the pouch from round the pirate's neck and open it. Inside you find six black pearls. Add 2 LUCK points. You leave the room with your valuable treasure. Outside in the corridor you may either open the other door if you have not done so already (turn to **232**) or leave the ship and continue your search of Port Blacksand, walking north up Harbour Street (turn to **78**).

112

While most of the houses in the street are small, cramped and dark, you see one ahead that stands alone and is painted bright red. The door has a 'Welcome' sign hanging from it. If you wish to enter the house, turn to **154**. If you prefer to keep walking north, turn to **334**.

113

You enter the house and find yourself standing in a room full of toys. But they are not ordinary toys. These are stuffed creatures with nails through their heads, dolls' houses that are made to look as if they are on fire, and many other unpleasant objects. In the middle of the room stand two old women dressed as though they were little girls. They are squabbling over a carved wooden duck. Each looks eager to destroy the duck with the knives they are holding. On seeing you the women both start to shout, 'Give us toys! Give us toys!' If you wish to give them something from your backpack, make the necessary deduction on your *Adventure Sheet* and turn to **141**. If you would rather leave these strange old ladies and continue east, turn to **375**.

114

There are three bejewelled rings under the counter and 13 Gold Pieces in a drawer. Take what you will and leave the shop to continue west (turn to **196**).

115

Coming towards you as fast as he is able is a man in tattered rags with a ball and chain attached to his leg. He is exhausted and collapses in your arms. His face is dirty and unshaven. With great difficulty he manages to speak, saying, 'Please cut me free. The town guards are not far behind me. I have been locked in a dungeon for two years but managed to tunnel my way out. I was robbed and unable to pay my taxes, so Lord Azzur ordered I should be jailed for five years. Please help me.' Farther up the street you hear shouting voices and then armed men come into view. If you want to cut through his chains with your sword, turn to **90**. If you want to hand him over to the town guards, turn to **274**.

116

Walking north along the street you see the entrance to a small herbalist's shop to your left. Looking through the window you see a wooden counter with a pair of scales upon it, and many sacks of different herbs crowding the floor. There is a small archway leading out of the back of the shop to another room. There is an 'Open' sign on the door but the shop is empty. If you wish to enter the shop, turn to **250**. If you would rather continue walking north up Market Street, turn to **93**.

117

At the end of the market, a street named Bridge Street runs north out of the square. You decide to walk down it in the hope of finding the elusive Nicodemus. It starts to rain and the tumbledown houses huddled together on either side of the street look as if they need shelter themselves. Most have their windows boarded up and are empty. The door to one flaps noisily in the wind. If you wish to take refuge in the derelict house until the rain stops, turn to **188**. If you would rather press on ahead, turn to **31**.

118

You can hear some scratching sounds in the tunnel ahead. Then you see a long shadow appear on the curved brick wall. In the dim light you can just make out the large shape of something black and shiny moving towards you. The scratching becomes louder and you also hear clicking sounds. The monster is only a couple of metres ahead of you when you recognize it as a Giant Centipede. Do you possess an insect bracelet? If you do, turn to **2**. If not, turn to **166**.

119

The small boy smiles and thrusts a tin mug into your hand. He tells you the barrel contains sparkling water which cures ills, wounds and diseases. To fill the mug costs 3 Gold Pieces. If you wish to drink the water, turn to **233**. If you would rather keep your gold and walk north, turn to **247**.

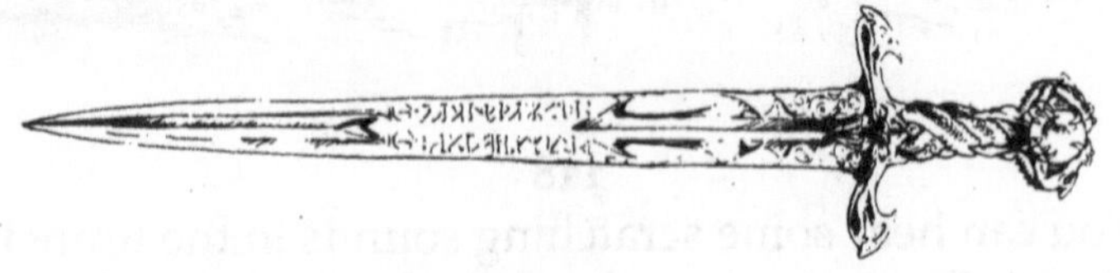

120

You pick up a piece of wood and run as quietly as possible over to the pirate to try to knock him unconscious. *Test your Luck*. If you are Lucky, he does not hear you approach and you hit him on the back of the head. He falls to the deck unconscious and you begin your search (turn to **84**). If you are Unlucky, you stumble on a coil of rope and the pirate turns to face you (turn to **152**).

121

The Ogre gulps down the food in no time at all. Licking his lips, he turns to you and tells you to get out of his home. If you wish to obey the ungrateful Ogre, and leave the house heading north, turn to **282**. If you wish to draw your sword to teach him a lesson, turn to **140**.

122

The room you enter is full of debris and rotting food. Standing in the middle of all the mess are two men wearing tattered clothing. They have hollow eyes and vacant expressions. On seeing you, they pick up wooden sticks and advance towards you. If you wish to back out of the room and shut them in, turn to **277**. If you wish to attack them, turn to **361**.

123

Inside a box on a wooden shelf you find 3 Gold Pieces and an iron key. On examining it you realize that it is a very special key. It is a skeleton key that will open just about any lock you care to try. Add 1 LUCK point and leave the shop to head west. Turn to **300**.

124

A narrow alleyway runs south off the street between two houses. If you wish to walk down the alleyway, turn to **326**. If you would rather continue along Harbour Street, turn to **180**.

125

This shield is cursed by Zanbar Bone. Anybody who is not undead will suffer if they use it. Lose 1 SKILL point. Unable to rid yourself of this handicap, you walk over to the spiral staircase and climb up it (turn to **21**).

126

The little girl grabs hold of your arm and leads you into a back room. Saying nothing, she motions you to lie down on a sheepskin rug. Suddenly you are aware of a very old man sitting opposite. He rises slowly from his rocking chair and walks over to you. You watch transfixed as he takes hold of an arrow protruding from your arm and gently pulls it free without causing you any pain. The wound made by the arrow disappears before your eyes. Other arrows are treated similarly if you suffered more than one wound. You may restore 2 STAMINA points for each arrow pulled free by the old man. Then in a slow and almost inaudible voice he tells you that he wants the broadsword that Owen Carralif gave you in payment for the healing. You feel obliged to give him your sword, though reluctantly. In exchange he gives you an ordinary fighting sword. Reduce your SKILL score by 1. You leave the house and head north (turn to **112**).

127

Just ahead of you, three men are involved in a fight – the two younger men appear to be attacking an older man with iron bars. If you wish to help the old man, turn to **177**. If you would rather avoid the brawling men and continue north, turn to **348**.

128

As you try to turn the lock with a piece of bent wire, you are alarmed by the sound of two clicks. Two tiny panels in the chest flick open to expose two needle darts which shoot out at you. *Test your Luck* twice, once for each dart. If you are Lucky both times, the darts bounce harmlessly off your armour (turn to **340**). If you are Unlucky once, a dart flies into your hand (turn to **149**). If you are Unlucky twice, both darts fly into your hand (turn to **19**).

129

You step back from the vile body of Zanbar Bone, waiting for him to decay. However, you have chosen wrongly! He pulls the arrow from his chest and rubs the compound from his eyes. He sees you and laughs. You are mesmerized by his power and are unable to move. He walks up to you and touches your face with his skeletal fingers. Your life is being quickly drained away, and soon you will begin your undead existence as a servant of Zanbar Bone.

130

As the guard slumps to the ground, two more armed men appear from a stone guardhouse by the gate, obviously attracted by the noise of your battle. There is no time to run so you must fight them one at a time.

	SKILL	STAMINA
First CITY GUARD	6	6
Second CITY GUARD	7	5

If you win, turn to 74.

131

You walk into a room with sparse furnishings and a polished wooden floor. Silk curtains hang down over an archway on the far wall. As you start to walk across the wooden floor, a woman's voice calls out 'Who is it?' You may:

Tell her you are delivering flowers	Turn to **67**
Tell her you have come to collect old rags	Turn to **6**
Tell her you are a tax collector	Turn to **179**

132

The creature pins the silver brooch to your leather tunic and you pay the price demanded. You have bought an item with healing properties. After surviving any battle, the brooch will immediately restore 1 STAMINA point to your total. Pleased with your purchase, you leave the house and head north (turn to **334**).

133

The street ends at a junction with Mill Street, which runs east and west along the city wall. Looking east you see a group of town guards marching towards you and you decide to walk quickly west along Mill Street. On your left you see a narrow lane and ahead you see a young lad coming towards you pushing a barrow laden with fruit. If you wish to walk down the lane, turn to **182**. If you wish to buy some fruit from the barrow-boy, turn to **160**.

134

You wake up feeling dazed, with a large lump on your head. Your backpack lies open by your side and you are annoyed to discover that all your gold has been stolen. Those thieving Dwarfs! You stand up and set off west down the street (turn to **396**).

135

When you draw your sword the man cries out and runs into a back room. You follow him into the room. He is apparently unarmed, but is holding an egg and a small key in his hands. He warns you that the egg contains a deadly gas and he will throw it at you. He also threatens to swallow the key to his silver cupboard. If you still wish to attack him, turn to **229**. If you wish to run out of the shop and go further up Clog Street, turn to **100**.

136

You walk over to the bar and order a drink. The old innkeeper scowls and tells you that he doesn't serve people from out of town. He pulls a dagger from his belt and, stabbing it in the bar top, tells you to leave. If you want to fight the innkeeper, turn to **270**. If you want to leave the tavern and head north, turn to **296**.

137

As you take your first step forwards you are alarmed to hear the familiar whistle of arrows flying through the air. They are coming from windows on either side of the street. Roll one die. This is the number of arrows that will hit you and each will cause you to lose 3 STAMINA points. If you are still alive, lose 2 LUCK points and turn to **327**.

138

If you fought the Ape Man, turn to **312**. If you fought any of the other creatures, turn to **283**.

139

Walking along the street you are suddenly halted by a plant pot smashing on to the cobblestones in front of you. You look to the left and see an open window. Inside, voices can be heard arguing. The door to the house is open. If you wish to enter the house to find out what the argument is about, turn to **113**. If you would rather ignore the argument and continue east, turn to **375**.

140

The OGRE looks unimpressed by your aggressive action and, picking up a large bone as a weapon, lumbers towards you. You must fight him.

OGRE	SKILL 8	STAMINA 9

If you defeat him, turn to **71**. After the third Attack Round, you may *Escape* by running out of the house to head north (turn to **282**).

141

The women immediately start arguing again over your gift to them, ignoring you completely. You look around the room and see a table set for a meal. There are two bowls of hot soup on top of the table waiting to be drunk. If you wish to pick up a wooden spoon and drink some of the soup, turn to **68**. If you would rather leave the old ladies and continue east, turn to **375**.

142

The crossbow bolt has a poisoned tip. You stagger back from the force of the bolt and fall to the ground. The poison spreads through your body quickly and you sink into a deep sleep from which you will not awaken.

143

When you hear the guards coming down the stairs, you lie on the floor and start to groan. They unlock the cell door and enter. If you wish to continue with your feigned illness and tell them that you think you've got the plague, turn to **306**. If you wish to fight them unarmed, turn to **157**.

144

The Hag screams as your sword cuts deep into her arm. Her concentration is lost and the spell is broken. Your mind clears and you are able to face her with your senses acute again. From out of her clothing the Hag pulls a dagger with a long shimmering blade. You are eager to fight her:

HAG	SKILL 7	STAMINA 7

If you win, turn to **303**.

145

Inside the shop an old woman is busily watering the flowers and plants. She looks up and smiles, saying, 'Good afternoon, my name is Mrs Pipe. Can I interest you in one of my special flowers?' If you wish to see what she has to offer, turn to **293**. If you wish to leave the shop, refuse politely and head west (turn to **24**).

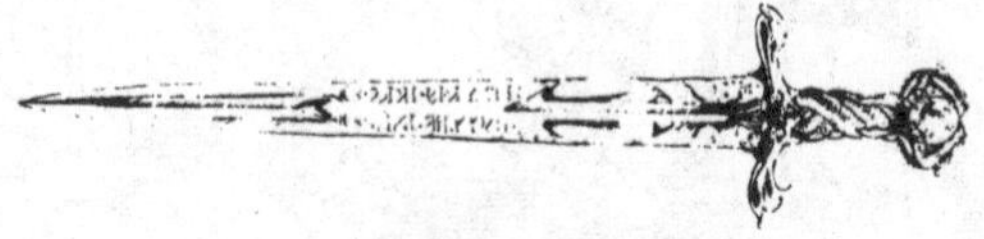

146

You walk back into the shop. You try to open the glass cupboard but it is locked. Inside you see two silver goblets, a silver chalice and a silver spoon. Do you have a skeleton key? If you have a key, turn to **220**. If you do not have a key, turn to **388**.

147

A search through the leather bags of the thieves produces 16 Gold Pieces and a glass phial containing a green liquid. If you wish to drink the liquid, turn to **338**. If you would rather just take the gold and press on northwards, turn to **105**.

ye
Goody-
Two-Shoes

148

As you catch up with the chanting crowd, you see that they are carrying eggs and rotten tomatoes. Soon the street opens out into a large market square. All round the edge are stalls with vendors, hawkers, musicians and entertainers carrying on their business. In the middle of the square is an elevated pillory. Above the noise of the crowd a trumpet sounds and the crowd start to pelt the man in the pillory with rotten food. An old woman standing next to you offers you two eggs to throw. Not wishing to appear to be an outsider, you take the eggs and hurl them. But as you do so, the old woman picks your pocket without you noticing. Lose 1 Gold Piece or any one item you may have. Unaware of your loss, you walk away from the crowd to look at the various stalls (turn to **287**).

149

The dart is poison-tipped. Lose 2 STAMINA points. If you are still alive and wish to continue picking the lock, turn to **340**. If you would rather leave the room and climb the stairs to the floor above, turn to **60**.

150

The Troll bursts out laughing and says, 'Fooled you! There isn't a Pepper Street in Port Blacksand!' His face folds into a sickly grin and he tells you that you are under arrest for being in Port Blacksand without authorization. He tells you that he is feeling generous, however, and offers you a choice. You can pay a fine of all the gold in your backpack and be thrown

out of the city, or spend a year with rats and cockroaches in a dirty dungeon cell. The other Troll bursts out laughing, saying, 'Generous? Ho! Ho! Ho! Ah, Sourbelly, you've got such a sense of humour!' If you wish to pay the fine and be thrown out of the city, turn to **367**. If you wish to resist arrest, turn to **73**.

151

The two guards lead you into the guardhouse and take you immediately downstairs to the cells below. There are four cells and all are empty except for one which houses a frail, white-haired old man. The guards unlock the cell next to the old man's and throw you in, placing your sword on a table outside. The only contents of the cell are a straw mattress and a pail of water. The guards go back upstairs and as they disappear the old man gets up off his bed and starts to speak. 'You're an outsider, aren't you? Don't reply, it's obvious. Do you want me to set you free? Give me 10 Gold Pieces and I'll have you out in five minutes.' The old man then puts his arm through the bars of your cell with the palm of his hand upturned. If you wish to give the old man 10 Gold Pieces, turn to **351**. If you would rather ignore the old man, turn to **29**.

152

The PIRATE draws his cutlass. As he approaches, his toothless grin unnerves you a little.

PIRATE	SKILL 7	STAMINA 5

You do not have time to draw your sword and must fight the pirate with the wooden stick. During each Attack Round you must deduct 2 points from your Attack Strength. If you win, turn to **20**.

153

Holding the golden owl in your hand, you are able to see into the pitch-black room. Just in time, you see the trip-wire across the doorway at your feet and the large crossbow pointing at you on the opposite wall. There is nothing else in the room. You decide to walk back to the staircase to climb up to the next floor (turn to **65**).

154

Inside the house you find yourself in a room painted red and empty apart from a table on top of which are two glass bowls. In one there is a small golden scorpion and in the other lies a silver scorpion. In the far corner of the room there are stairs that lead up to another floor. You may:

Pick up the golden scorpion	Turn to **273**
Pick up the silver scorpion	Turn to **13**
Climb the stairs	Turn to **80**
Leave the house and head north	Turn to **334**

155

Lose 3 STAMINA points. If you are still alive, you stand up and brush yourself down. The carriage races out of view and you set off west again, hoping that you will have another opportunity to meet the infamous Lord Azzur (turn to **171**).

156

Standing on either side of you, the Trolls march you along Mill Street until you reach the city's North Gate at the junction with Goose Street. They tell the two guards on duty not to let you back into Port Blacksand. They give you a forceful boot up the backside and you land sprawling on the dusty road outside. Do you have all the items required to slay the Night Prince? If you have them all and have been tattooed, turn to **201**. If you are missing any of the items or have not been tattooed, turn to **299**.

157

You leap up and punch the first guard. He staggers back and draws his sword. You fight them one at a time in the small cell.

	SKILL	STAMINA
First CITY GUARD	6	6
Second CITY GUARD	7	5

During each Attack Round you must deduct 3 from your Attack Strength because you are fighting bare-handed. If you manage to defeat the guards, you leave the cell and climb the stairs, picking up your sword off the table (turn to **54**).

158

You must react quickly to escape the advancing Suit of Armour. If you wish to open the door in front of you, turn to **122**. If you wish to run back to the staircase and climb up to the next floor, turn to **207**.

159

The owner of the house is obviously quite wealthy. Lavish furnishing and fine *objets d'art* adorn the marble-floored room in which you stand. An archway leads into a back room and stairs to your right lead up to another floor. Will you:

Search the room you are in?	Turn to **278**
Walk through the archway?	Turn to **107**
Climb the stairs?	Turn to **60**

160

The boy puts down his barrow and asks you what you would like to buy. He recommends his plums as being particularly refreshing. If you wish to pay 1 Gold Piece for a bag of plums, turn to **211**. If you wish to buy a bag of red apples for 1 Gold Piece, turn to **242**.

161

The street makes a sudden left turn and continues north as far as you can see. However, you notice that round the corner the houses are much bigger, with doorways some four metres high. On the left side of the street you see that a door to one of the houses is open. If you wish to enter the house, turn to **245**. If you wish to keep going northwards, turn to **282**.

162

Test your Luck. If you are Lucky, you manage to cut the pouch loose without waking the pirates (turn to **7**). If you are Unlucky, the man's eyes flick open as you try to cut the cord and he grabs hold of your arm while calling out to his mates for help (turn to **226**).

163

The sarcophagus contains a gold ring which has an eye etched into its top. You have found the long-lost Ring of the Golden Eye, fabled for its ability to allow its wearer to detect illusions. Add 2 LUCK points and leave the room (turn to **231**).

164

You stagger forward beyond the angle of fire of the unseen archers. Ahead you see some sacks lying outside a house and you slump down on top of them. Slowly and painfully you pull the arrows from your body. After bandaging your wounds you rise to your feet and continue north (turn to **112**).

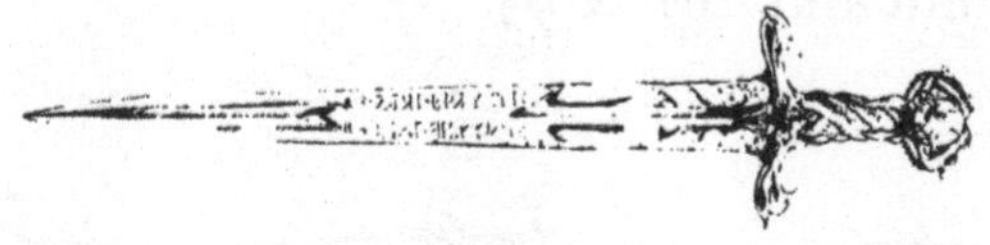

165

You may either turn right down Candle Street (turn to **139**) or walk back to the junction and go down Harbour Street (turn to **91**).

166

You will have to swing your sword with all your might to pierce the armour-like shell of this monster.

GIANT CENTIPEDE SKILL 10 STAMINA 5

If you win, turn to **272**.

167

When you have paid the Man-Orc the 4 Gold Pieces, he explains that placing the herbs on a wound will help to heal it. Unfortunately the strength of the mixture varies. When required, roll 1 die. The number rolled is the number of STAMINA points that will be restored. Somewhat surprised at your good fortune you leave the shop and walk north. Add 1 LUCK point and turn to **93**.

168

The Bays have difficulty in explaining themselves, but you manage to understand that one of the other team is going to throw the ball at you. You are handed the wooden stick and told that if you hit the ball over the wall, you will win the game for them. Roll two dice. If the number rolled is equal to or less than your SKILL score, you hit the ball powerfully in the middle of the bat and watch it soar over the wall (turn to **359**). If the number rolled is greater than your SKILL score, the ball goes whistling by your midriff as you swing, and a voice behind you calls, 'You're out!' (turn to **266**).

169

The blacksmith removes his gloves and wipes his hands on his apron before asking you what you want. You answer by asking if he makes anything besides horseshoes. He replies that in his spare time he enjoys making chainmail coats. In fact it has become quite a profitable sideline of his, especially in a place like Port Blacksand. He tells you in great detail of the skill and labour that goes into making one and finally inquires if you are interested in buying one. They are not cheap. If you wish to pay 20 Gold Pieces for a chainmail coat, turn to **46**. If you wish to leave the stables without buying a coat, turn to **115**.

170

The man sees you drawing your sword and snatches his battle-axe off the wall. He walks around the counter to fight you.

JEWELLER	SKILL 9	STAMINA 8

If you win, turn to **114**. You may *Escape* by running out of the shop and west along the street (turn to **196**).

171

The street gradually starts to run downhill. The houses end at a tavern called the Black Lobster and the street opens out on to a quayside. A stone jetty runs out to sea and tied to it is an old galleon. It is flying the skull and crossbones and is probably one of the many pirate ships that anchor in Port Blacksand to off-load their booty. Harbour Street turns right at the jetty and runs north parallel to the shore as far as you can see. If you wish to walk down the jetty to climb on board the ship, turn to **399**. If you wish to walk north up Harbour Street, turn to **78**.

172

You take the bunch of flowers out of your backpack and hand it to the Serpent Queen. She thanks you and hands you a tip of 2 Gold Pieces before showing you to the front door. Outside you set off north along Stable Street (turn to **333**).

173

The three old bearded Dwarfs are so involved with their game that they pay you no attention as you sit down at their table. Finally, one turns to you and asks if you would like to join in their game. If you wish to gamble some of your Gold Pieces, turn to **206**. If you would rather leave the smoky tavern and walk north, turn to **296**.

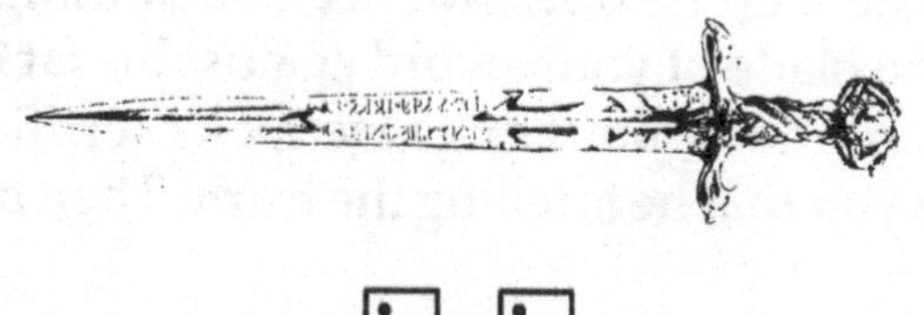

174

Back at the entrance hole you may either climb up the ladder to the street in order to continue east (turn to **205**) or, if you have not done so already, you may walk north along the sewer (turn to **356**).

175

Slowly lifting the goblet, you are surprised to see a yellow scorpion underneath. It darts forward and tries to sting you on the hand with its poisonous tail. *Test your Luck*. If you are Lucky, the tail stabs the goblet (turn to **204**). If you are Unlucky, the barb on its tail sinks into your hand (turn to **373**).

176

You tell the worried bather that, despite your hatred for pirates, you will not harm him if he cooperates with you. You ask him if he has any of the items that you are searching for, but he replies that as captain of a pirate ship he does not need such things. You press the blade of your sword against his fat neck to make sure he is not lying. He looks terrified and assures you that he is telling the truth. Then he says,

'But I do know where you can get a silver arrow. Ben Borryman the silversmith will make anything in silver at a price. You will find him in Clog Street.' Making a mental note of the information you leave the shivering captain alone in his room, locking the door behind you. Outside in the corridor you may either open the other door if you have not done so already (turn to **271**) or leave the ship and continue your search of Port Blacksand by walking north up Harbour Street (turn to **78**).

177

You draw your sword and rush to help the old man. He is lying on the ground and the other two men are beating him and trying to take his leather bag. You call out and they turn and attack you.

	SKILL	STAMINA
First ROBBER	7	8
Second ROBBER	8	6

Fight them one at a time. If you win, turn to **51**.

178

The archway leads into a large room in the centre of which crouches a human-like creature, some three metres tall. He looks very worried and is muttering to himself. The lumps on his face are the distinguishing marks of an Ogre. Will you:

Attempt to speak with him?	Turn to **264**
Attack him with your sword?	Turn to **140**
Leave the house to head north?	Turn to **282**

179

The silk curtains in front of the archway are pulled aside and a brown leather bag flies out and lands in front of you, making a dull jingling sound. If you wish to open the bag, turn to **16**. If you wish to leave the house without opening the bag and continue north along Stable Street, turn to **333**.

180

Ahead you hear the noisy clatter of galloping hooves on the cobblestones. You hear the noise of wooden wheels and an urging voice followed by the crack of a whip. Someone is rapidly approaching in a horse-drawn carriage; if you wish to see who it is, turn to **344**. If you would rather hide out of sight behind a barrel and watch the carriage pass by, turn to **34**.

181

The key fits the lock and the handle turns. Turn to **159**.

MOTHER

182

The lane ends at a small shop. On the glass-paned door is painted a sign: 'Jimmy Quicktint, Best Tattooist in Town'. A tiny bell rings as you push the door open and a fat man wearing purple silk smiles in greeting. You are surprised to see that his arms, hands, feet and even his face are completely covered in colourful tattoos. He grins and says, 'Practise what you preach!' You tell him that you require a yellow sun to be tattooed on your forehead with a white unicorn in the centre of it. He replies that it is a simple task but it will cost you 10 Gold Pieces. If you can afford his high price, turn to **279**. If you cannot, turn to **354**.

183

You are told that smoking mixture and a pipe costs 1 Gold Piece, and healing mixture costs 4 Gold Pieces per portion. You may:

Buy some smoking mixture	Turn to **366**
Buy some healing mixture	Turn to **167**
Leave the shop and head north	Turn to **93**

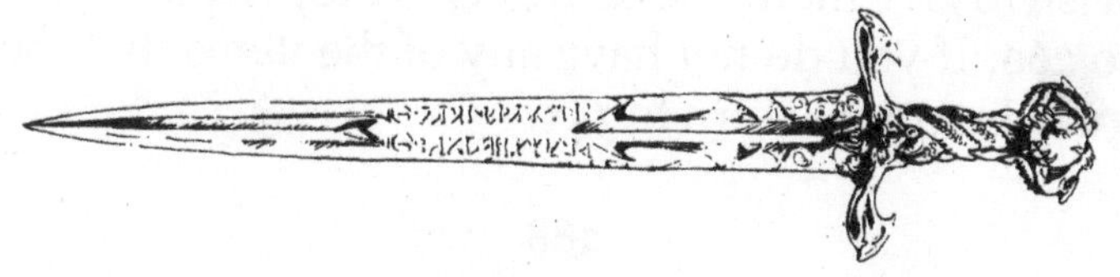

184

Do you have any of Mrs Pipe's golden flowers? If you do, turn to **55**. If not, turn to **308**.

185

The suit of armour breaks up as it crashes on to the floor. It is no threat to you and you may either open the door in front of you (turn to **122**) or walk back to the staircase and climb up to the next floor (turn to **207**).

186

On top of the Lizardine's table you find 4 Gold Pieces and a scorpion brooch made of copper. If you wish to pick up the brooch and pin it to your tunic, turn to **387**. If you would rather just take the gold, go back down the stairs and leave the house, heading north, turn to **334**.

187

You tell the town guards that you have something special for them if they let the two of you go. They reply that the prisoner is a murderer and that you should not help him, but they insist that you bribe them or else you too will be taken to the jail. They say they are interested in any of the following items: magic armour, magic rings or magic potions. If you wish to give them one of the items they require, turn to **260**. If you do not have any of the items that the guards require, turn to **341**.

188

It is gloomy in the house but you can make out the shapes of abandoned furniture. Litter and rubble is strewn all over the floor. You find a broken chair and slump down in it to rest. Suddenly you notice something slither across the floor, and before you can get to your feet you see in the half-light that you are encircled by six snakes, each a metre long. If you wish to hack at them with your sword, turn to **253**. If you would rather make a dash for the door, turn to **15**.

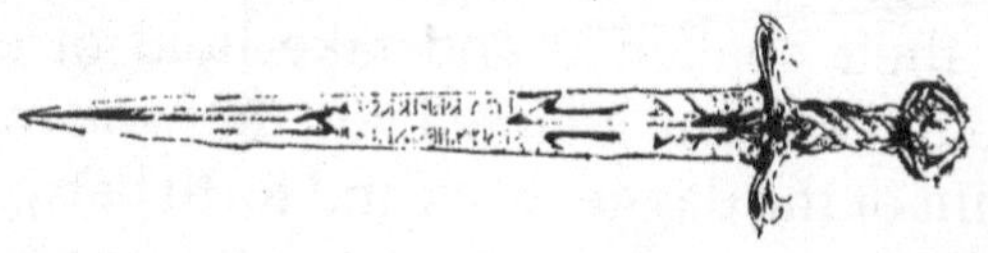

189

You take aim with your bow and fire the arrow at the Spirit Stalker. The arrow plunges into its chest and the agonized look on the face of the Spirit Stalker tells you that the arrow has pierced its heart. It falls to the floor, and smoke starts to rise from its rotten flesh. Its mouth opens to release a deafening howl that echoes around the hallway and makes you shudder. Finally it is still, and you retrieve your silver arrow. You see that you are in a beautiful marble-floored hallway. On three of the four walls hang portraits of evil-looking men and women, but on the far wall hang two iron shields. The crest on one is a tower, and on the other a unicorn. A spiral staircase leads up from the centre of the hallway to the floor above. Will you:

Take the shield with the tower crest?	Turn to **125**
Take the shield with the unicorn crest?	Turn to **374**
Climb the spiral staircase?	Turn to **21**

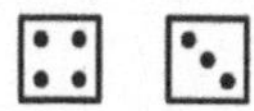

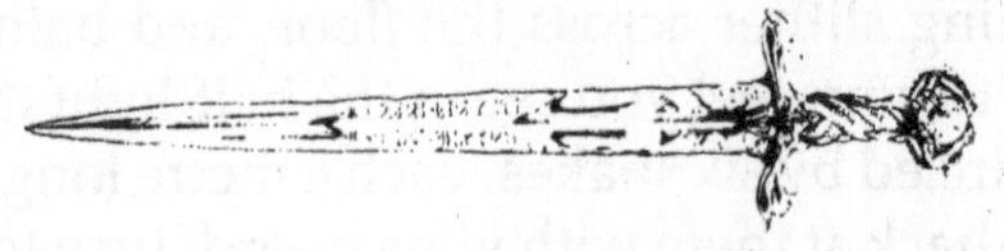

190

Sitting down at the table the men invite you to join in their game of pin-finger. You feel obliged to accept their challenge and take hold of a dagger offered to you. The men tell you that you must stick the point of the dagger back and forth between your fingers into the table top as fast as you can for a minute. If you manage not to stab yourself they will give you a magic item. If you do stab yourself you must give them 5 Gold Pieces. Roll two dice. If the number rolled is less than or equal to your SKILL score, you succeed (turn to **38**). If the number rolled is greater than your SKILL, you are unable to control the fast movement of the dagger and stab one of your fingers. You toss 5 Gold Pieces on the table and stand up to leave the tavern. Outside you head north again (turn to **296**).

191

You draw your sword to defend yourself against the advancing LEAF BEASTS. They all attack you at once, seemingly trying to crush and smother you. Treat the Leaf Beasts as a single creature.

LEAF BEASTS	SKILL 6	STAMINA 6

If you win, you run back to the turnstile still clutching the lotus and make your getaway into Stable Street (turn to **133**).

192

It is a drop of some five metres to the ground and you land heavily. *Test your Luck*. If you are Lucky, you escape injury and set off north again (turn to **304**). If you are Unlucky, you twist your sword arm badly. Lose 1 SKILL point. Once again, you head north (turn to **304**).

193

If you have a Ring of Fire, it will be the best weapon against the Mummy (turn to **286**). Otherwise you must use your sword.

MUMMY	SKILL 7	STAMINA 12

If you win, turn to **163**.

194

The smoke in the glass ball appears to vanish as you place it carefully in your backpack. Feeling slightly uneasy about your new treasure you set off east again (turn to **161**).

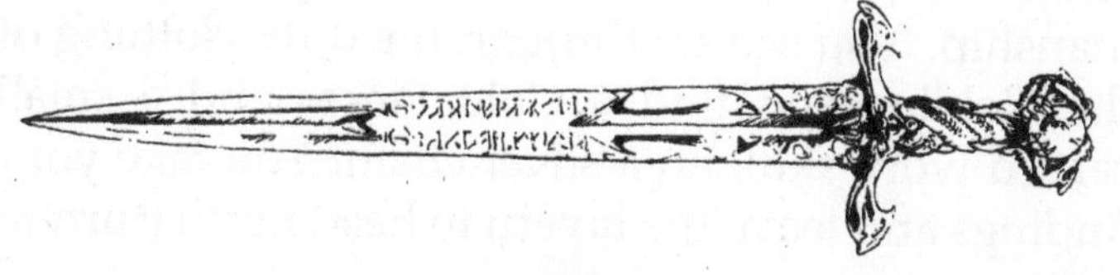

195

Which person will you say sent the flowers? You may:

Tell her it is Lord Azzur	Turn to **61**
Tell her it is Mrs Pipe	Turn to **268**
Tell her it is Ben Borryman	Turn to **53**

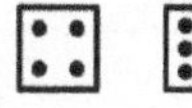

196

You arrive at a four-way junction in the street. The street continuing west changes its name to Key Street, and the street running north and south is called Market Street. Looking north you see a crowd of people walking up the street cheering loudly and waving their arms in the air. You decide to follow them (turn to **148**).

197

On the next landing there is a door with a black tower carved in ebony attached to it. There is also a black suit of armour standing outside the door. Will you:

Inspect the suit of armour?	Turn to **301**
Open the door?	Turn to **122**
Carry on up the stairs?	Turn to **207**

198

You look around at the rest of the crowd but they remain seated out of respect for your swordsmanship. You search through the dirty clothing of the Goblins and find 9 Gold Pieces and a small carved ivory skull on a silver chain. You take your findings and leave the tavern to head north (turn to **296**).

199

You tell the town guards that you are a bounty hunter. They seem pleased that you have caught their wanted man. The chief guard walks over to you and hands you 5 Gold Pieces, saying, 'This murderer won't escape again. Here's your reward.' He then rejoins the other guards who are busy chaining up the escaped murderer. You decide to head quickly north in case the murderer tries to implicate you (turn to **222**).

200

In the next stall area there is a small, brightly coloured tent. Attached to it is a small sign which reads, 'Madame Star, Clairvoyant'. If you wish to enter the tent, turn to **394**. If you would rather continue north, turn to **117**.

201

Following Nicodemus's map, you start your long walk north to the guarded tower of Zanbar Bone, the Night Prince. You walk through woods and fields. You are able to relax a little in the pleasant countryside and breathe the fresh air with its wonderful scents. As the light fades you decide to camp under a huge elm tree. You cook a meal of stewed rabbit and mushrooms before settling down to a long, deep sleep (add 2 STAMINA points). In the morning you look around for a yew tree and cut a long branch from it with which you make a bow to fire the silver arrow. As you test the bow for accuracy, you are suddenly aware of a white dove sitting

on a low branch near by. There is a small piece of paper attached to its foot which it lets you remove without flying off. There is a message on the paper which reads:

Dear Friend,
I am afraid I must be getting too old to be of use to anybody. I regret that I have misinformed you about the compound needed to kill Zanbar Bone. You must use only two of the three ingredients I told you, but I cannot remember which two. I can only suggest you try Hag's hair and black pearls together, or the Hag's hair and lotus flower together, or the black pearls and lotus flower together. Apologies.
Good luck,
N.

You throw the message on the ground and curse. You change your mind a dozen times before making a decision. Finally you make your choice, and grind the two ingredients together on a flat stone. You place the compound in a leather pouch, hoping you have made the correct decision. You set off again, but it is not long before your surroundings become less welcoming, the trees are twisted or stunted and there are no birds to be heard – you must be approaching the domain of the Night Prince. Suddenly to your left you hear rustling and grunting in the bushes. It is a wandering monster which has been attracted by your scent. Roll one die and consult the table below to see what creature has appeared. Fight this creature as usual.

Die roll	Creature	SKILL	STAMINA
1	ORC	5	4
2	GIANT SNAKE	6	6
3	WOLF	5	5
4	PYGMY	4	4
5	APE MAN	7	6
6	CAVE TROLL	8	7

If you win, turn to **138**.

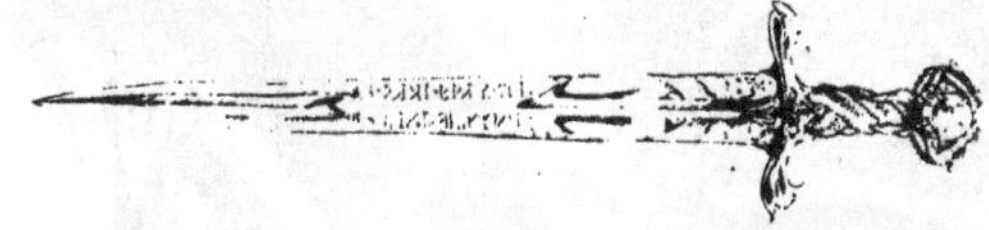

202

The guard replies that he will send for an escort to take you to Nicodemus. He reaches up to a small bell on the wall of the guardhouse and rings it three times. Almost immediately two other guards come running out of the house, and you are surprised when they each grab hold of one of your arms. The guard with the pike looks up to the sky and laughs, saying, 'So you want to see Nicodemus, do you? How would you like to see the inside of a dungeon cell instead? Guards, take this fool away to be shackled, and throw away the key.' Will you:

Allow yourself to be taken away? Turn to **151**
Attempt to fight the guards? Turn to **69**
Try to bribe the guards? Turn to **276**

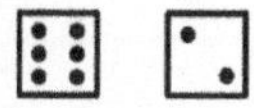

203

Zanbar Bone walks towards you, trying to touch your exposed skin. You throw down your sword and notch the silver arrow to your bow. You have only one chance. You take aim and release the bow-string. *Test your Luck.* If you are Lucky, the arrow finds its mark and pierces the Night Prince through his robed chest (turn to **244**). If you are Unlucky, the arrow misses the Night Prince and he advances to touch your arm. His skeletal fingers are draining your life away. You are now one of his undead servants.

204

You drop the goblet and pull your hand away. The scorpion scurries a metre across the floor before you step on it with your boot. If you have not done so already, you may lift goblet B (turn to **209**) or goblet C (turn to **43**). If you have lost interest in the goblets, you may either walk through the archway (turn to **107**) or climb the stairs (turn to **60**).

205

After replacing the manhole cover you set off east again. Everything seems a little too quiet and you begin to feel nervous. Ahead you see that Stable Street turns sharply to the left. If you wish to walk round the corner, turn to **44**. If you wish to walk back to the junction and turn right into Tower Street, turn to **127**.

206

The Dwarf explains that they are playing a simple winner-takes-all dice game. The stakes are 2 Gold Pieces. Each person will stake 2 Gold Pieces and roll two dice. The person rolling the highest number collects the 8 Gold Pieces. To play, roll two dice three times for the three Dwarfs and make a note of each total. Next, roll two dice for yourself. If your own total is higher than each of the other three totals, you win 6 Gold Pieces from the Dwarfs. If the total is less than any of the other three totals, you lose 2 Gold Pieces. You may play four times if you wish to before the Dwarfs get bored and leave the tavern. At the end of the game you leave the tavern yourself to head north (turn to **296**).

207

The staircase ends at a door. You turn the handle slowly and the door opens, much to your surprise, into open air. You walk outside on to the flat roof of the tower. Suddenly you are aware of movement in the sky and look up to see two large birds in the moonlight with long beaks and talons swooping down on you. There is no time to run for cover, and you must fight the DEATH HAWKS.

	SKILL	STAMINA
First DEATH HAWK	4	5
Second DEATH HAWK	4	4

Fight them one at a time. If you win, turn to **314**.

208

The Goblin's pockets contain 2 Gold Pieces, a clove of garlic and some old knucklebones. Take what you wish and head east again along Clog Street (turn to 317).

209

Underneath the goblet lies a small pile of Gold Pieces. You count 12 in all and put them in your backpack. If you have not done so already, you may lift goblet A (turn to 175) or goblet C (turn to 43). If you are not interested in the goblets, you may either walk through the archway (turn to 107) or climb the stairs (turn to 60).

210

Her gaze is so hypnotic that you are unable to look away. You are defenceless and cannot resist as she embraces you and slowly sinks her fangs into your neck to drink your blood. You drift into an unconscious sleep, and when you awake you are unaware of your previous existence – you have become a Vampire yourself!

211

The plums are sweet and juicy and taste delicious. Add 1 STAMINA point. You wipe your mouth with the back of your hand and continue west (turn to 307).

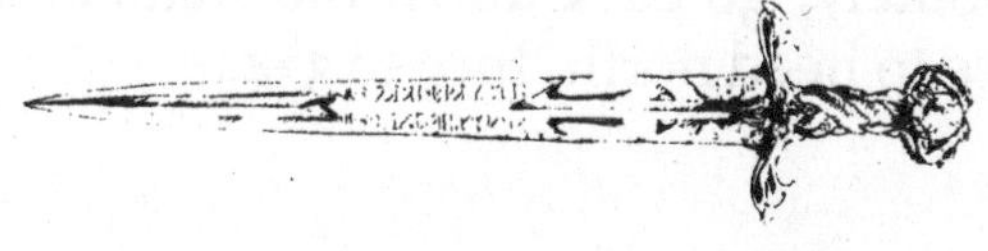

212

You are relieved that the noise of your fight did not attract any more guards, but not wishing to tempt providence you dash into the city (turn to **74**).

213

A man wearing a white apron is sitting at a bench busily polishing a silver goblet. There are several silver objects in a glass cupboard secured by an iron grill at the back of the shop. You may:

Talk to the silversmith	Turn to **248**
Attack him with your sword	Turn to **135**
Leave the shop and continue east	Turn to **100**

214

As soon as you touch the battle-axe, the Suit of Armour starts to move. In a series of quick, jerky movements it swings the battle-axe in an attempt to strike you. *Test your Luck.* If you are Lucky, you manage to jump back out of reach of the swinging axe (turn to **158**). If you are Unlucky, the blade cuts into your left arm (turn to **379**).

215

The lizard-like creature starts to speak in a low, hissing voice by asking whether you would like to buy one of its famous scorpion brooches. If you wish to buy one, turn to **315**. If you would rather refuse politely, go back down the stairs and leave the house to head north, turn to **334**.

216

Clog Street is very narrow and lined with terraced cottages and the occasional shop. To your left you see what looks like a small boy lying face down on the cobblestones, groaning loudly. A hood is pulled over his head and you cannot see his face. A wooden hoop and stick lie by his side. If you wish to stop to help, turn to **72**. If you would rather walk on, turn to **317**.

217

You walk all day until you reach the hill shown on Nicodemus's map upon which the Night Prince's tower stands. All is quiet and there is an unpleasant smell of decay in the air. Shadows start to creep along the ground as the moon rises into the night sky and you see the foreboding silhouetted shape of Zanbar Bone's tower pointing up into the sky like a black finger. You check all your possessions before drawing your sword and marching towards the arched wooden entrance door. Suddenly you hear a shrill howl and swing round to see two pairs of eyes staring at you. They belong to MOON DOGS, Zanbar Bone's trained killer hounds. Fight them one at a time.

	SKILL	STAMINA
First MOON DOG	9	10
Second MOON DOG	11	9

If you win, turn to **259**.

218

The Dwarf smiles and extends his arm to you, saying, 'An enemy of Nicodemus is a friend of mine. Welcome stranger.' You tell Wraggins that you do not know where Nicodemus lives and he explains that the wizard lives alone in a small hut under Singing Bridge, which crosses Catfish River to the old part of the city and harbour. He explains that the bridge is in the middle of the city and that most streets lead to it. You thank the Dwarf for his information and leave his shop to continue west along Key Street (turn to **300**).

219

The larger of the two Trolls tells you that his name is Sourbelly and it is his duty to track down unwelcome visitors to Port Blacksand. He looks at the pass and says, 'You don't look much like a merchant to me. Are you one of those fancy folk who have been attending the spice sales in Pepper Street?' If you wish to answer 'Yes', turn to **150**. If you wish to answer 'No', turn to **393**.

220

The key fits the lock securing the grill enclosing the glass cupboard. It clicks open and you are able to take any of the items you wish. You find nothing else of interest in the shop, so you walk outside and continue east (turn to **100**).

221

The alley is narrow and dark and runs south some twenty metres before coming to a dead end at a wall. The Dwarfs are nowhere to be seen. You start walking slowly back up the alley when suddenly a large net falls on you from above. It is weighted and you stumble to the ground, completely entangled. Then you become aware of the three Dwarfs standing above you, chuckling to themselves. Their hands reach through the netting and you watch helplessly as they rummage through your backpack. They seem interested only in your gold. Eventually they walk off and leave you to wriggle free. You have lost all your gold. Lose 2 LUCK points. Returning to the street, you turn left and head west (turn to **396**).

222

On the right-hand side the houses are separated from the street by a wooden fence with shrubs, trees, bushes and flowers behind it. There is a turnstile in the middle of the fence, by the side of which is a sign reading: 'Public Gardens. Entry Fee 1 Gold Piece'. If you wish to go into the gardens, turn to **370**. If you would rather keep on walking, turn to **133**.

J. WRAGGINS
LOCKSMITH.

223

Sweat breaks out on your forehead – you choose a pill and swallow it. Roll one die. If you roll any number between 2 and 6, you have chosen a harmless pill. The man reaches into a pouch on his cord belt and hands you 20 Gold Pieces. He then bids you farewell and tells you to come back soon. You leave the room and walk back up the alley to Candle Street (turn to **165**). A roll of 1 means you die quickly from the poisoned pill and your adventure ends here.

224

Sitting on a stool at the back of the shop is an old bespectacled Dwarf. He is busy cutting a key on a cast-iron treadle machine which squeaks and grinds noisily. You cough to get his attention, but he does not look up from his work. Finally the machine comes to a halt and the Dwarf asks you what you want. You may either ask him if he has any skeleton keys for sale (turn to **66**) or ask him if he knows where Nicodemus lives (turn to **236**).

225

Each VAGABOND boasts that he can kill you singlehanded. They decide to fight you one at a time.

	SKILL	STAMINA
First VAGABOND	7	5
Second VAGABOND	6	7
Third VAGABOND	5	6

If you win, turn to **397**.

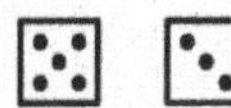

226

You manage to break free from the pirate's grip and draw your sword. You step backwards towards the door as the PIRATES leap from their bunks to grab their cutlasses. The room is cramped and you fight them one at a time.

	SKILL	STAMINA
First PIRATE	6	6
Second PIRATE	5	4
Third PIRATE	7	4

If you win, turn to **111**. You may *Escape* by backing out through the door and fleeing from the ship north up Harbour Street (turn to **78**).

227

The street soon makes another sharp turn to the right and you find yourself walking east. Outside one of the houses to your left is a pile of rubbish and broken objects. On top of the pile is a pair of old boots that look about your size. If you wish to try them on, turn to **362**. If you wish to keep walking east, turn to **103**.

228

The key fits the lock, which clicks open as you turn it. You open the door and enter a beautiful marble-floored hallway. On three of the four walls hang portraits of evil-looking men and women, but on the far wall hang two iron shields. The crest on one is a tower and on the other a unicorn. A spiral staircase leads up from the centre of the hallway to a floor above. Will you:

Take the shield with the tower crest?	Turn to **125**
Take the shield with the unicorn crest?	Turn to **374**
Climb the spiral staircase?	Turn to **21**

229

As you advance towards him the man swallows the key and throws the egg at you. *Test your Luck*. If you are Lucky, the egg misses you and breaks against a wall to release a green-coloured gas (turn to **23**). If you are Unlucky, the egg breaks against your chest and you breathe in some of the green-coloured gas released (turn to **343**).

230

You scratch around in the cracks in the wall and find a loose stone. The old man watches intently as you pull the stone out of the wall. Peering into the hole you see an iron key. You place it in the lock of your cell and are amazed to feel it turn. Add 1 LUCK point. With the cell door open you put the key back in the hole in the wall and replace the stone. You leave your cell and pick up your sword off the table. Then you call out to the guards, telling them that you think they are stupid and that you have seen more life on a Troll's breakfast plate than in them. Quickly provoked, the GUARDS rush down the stairs and

are surprised to see you waiting for them, sword drawn. You fight them one at a time.

	SKILL	STAMINA
First CITY GUARD	6	6
Second CITY GUARD	7	5

If you win, you climb the stairs (turn to **54**).

231

Outside on the landing you may either enter the black door (turn to **96**) or walk back to the stairs to climb up to the next floor (turn to **197**).

232

The door opens into a small room, in the centre of which stands a steaming tub of hot water. If you wish to hide behind the door inside the room to see who is about to take a bath, turn to **12**. If you would rather close the door, turn to **383**.

233

The sparkling water is refreshing but not as medicinal as the small boy claimed. Add 1 STAMINA point to your total. You shake your fist at the boy in mock anger, and set off north (turn to **247**).

234

The tiny man smiles and says, 'Ah well, if that's all you want, then that's simple enough. He's on the fourth floor in the room with the black door.' Then he waves his arms at you and disappears in a small puff of smoke. You stand up and walk back down the stairs to the floor where there are two doors adjacent to each other on the landing. You breathe in deeply and turn the handle of the black door (turn to **96**).

235

You decide not to risk any further possible danger to yourself and crawl out of the room. You stand up, walk over to the staircase and climb up to the next floor (turn to **65**).

236

Your question produces a suspicious look on the face of the Dwarf and he raises one eyebrow. Then he says, 'I know Nicodemus but what do you want of him?' You may reply by telling him either that you are on a mission from Silverton and need the help of Nicodemus (turn to **57**), or that you want to kill Nicodemus (turn to **218**).

237

You rub the jewel in the ring and point it at the Leaf Beasts. A blast of fire shoots out of the ring and burns a large hole in the nearest Leaf Beast. It makes a whistling cry and backs away. You seize your opportunity and dash through their broken defence. You run to the turnstile clutching the lotus and make your escape into Stable Street (turn to **133**).

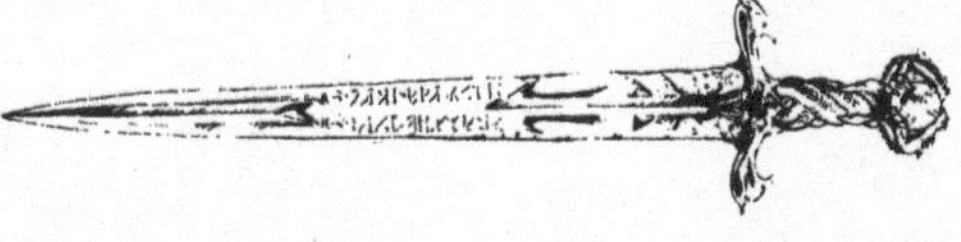

Goose Street

238

On the right side of the street you see a small alleyway between two houses. The alley soon ends at a doorway with six skulls painted on it; one black and five white. If you wish to walk down the alley and open the door, turn to **27**. If you would rather continue east, turn to **139**.

239

Behind you comes the sound of running feet. You look round and see a group of town guards chasing after you. As you stop to think where to run next, a boy runs out of a house and shouts, 'Follow me!' You have no better plan in mind so you run after him. The boy races down to the bottom of Mill Street and turns left into Goose Street. He stops at a cart laden with hay and starts to talk frantically to a kind-faced old man, saying, 'Uncle! Uncle! This brave person killed Sourbelly. We must help him to escape.' The old man speaks calmly to the boy, saying, 'Indeed we owe our friend a favour. Quick, jump into the cart.' You climb into the cart and cover yourself with hay. You lie completely motionless as you hear the running guards approach. They stop to speak to the old thatcher, but he sends them running off down Goose Street. After they are gone he whispers to you that he will take you to safety. You hear him climb on to the cart and urge his horse into a slow trot. The cart bounces noisily along the cobbled street but you feel comfortable in the hay. The cart stops and starts a few times, and you hear questioning voices. About half an hour later the cart

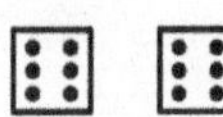

stops again and the thatcher calls out, 'You can come out now.' You poke your head out of the hay and are surprised to see that you are on the edge of a wood. To the west you can see the daunting shape of Port Blacksand. You jump out of the cart and thank the thatcher for his trouble. He says goodbye to you and wheels his cart round to return to Port Blacksand. Do you have all the items required to slay the Night Prince, and have you been tattooed? If you have, turn to **201**. If you are missing any of the items, or have not been tattooed, turn to **299**.

240

The man hands you the gold and puts the gems under the counter. If you now wish to inquire about the price of his rings, turn to **36**. If you have had enough of transactions for the time being, you leave the shop and head west (turn to **196**).

241

Inside the shop you see a tall, thin man with pointed ears and fair hair, pouring hot wax from an iron pan into a mould. The candle-maker is an Elf. As he turns to you to speak, you notice his slanted eyes, which are ice blue. For some reason they appear very cold to you. He tells you that all his coloured candles cost 1 Gold Piece each. You may buy as many as you wish. He then asks you if you would like to see one of his magic candles in the back room. If you wish to see one, turn to **63**. If you would rather leave the shop and head east, turn to **280**.

242

The boy hurriedly picks up his barrow and dashes off, saying he is late for market. You eat an apple but it is sour. Your stomach starts to hurt and the pain develops into cramp. You do not feel very well at all. Lose 1 STAMINA point. You throw the other apples away and continue west (turn to 307).

243

You have suffered a terrible burn. Lose 5 STAMINA points. If you are still alive, you decide to lie still and feign death. Behind you the fat man is still chortling to himself. You hear him walk over to you and then feel a sharp pain as he kicks you in the ribs. Satisfied that you really are dead, he walks up the stairs. In considerable pain, you crawl along the floor to the door. Without making a sound you crawl outside. Hauling yourself to your feet you stagger off up the street (turn to 304).

244

The Night Prince is paralysed, but not for long. He can summon unearthly powers to defend himself, and you must act quickly. What compound will you rub into his eyes? Will you try:

Hag's hair and black pearls?	Turn to **9**
Black pearls and lotus flower?	Turn to **129**
Lotus flower and Hag's hair?	Turn to **337**

245

You enter a large room with brown walls and a straw-covered floor. There is a musty smell hanging in the air which reminds you of the dirty old Cave Trolls that live on the northern borders. In the middle of the room is a table made from half a barrel with some roughly made stools round it. A high archway leads through the room to the back of the house, from where you hear a low murmuring voice. If you want to walk through the archway, turn to **178**. If you wish to leave the house and continue north, turn to **282**.

246

As you walk warily down the narrow cobbled street, you are suddenly confronted by a little old man who dashes out of one of the houses. He pulls a dirty bottle out of a canvas bag. As he speaks, you can't help staring at the large wart on his nose, with its tuft of hair. He smiles and asks if you would like to pay 2 Gold Pieces for a drink of his wonderful healing potion. If you wish to pay for a drink, turn to **98**. If you would rather keep going east, turn to **363**.

247

The street makes a sharp turn to the left and continues west for some distance. Turning the corner, you are suddenly jumped on by three short, stocky assailants who were hiding down an alley. Two grab your legs and one tries to knock you out with a cudgel. *Test your Luck*. If you are Lucky, you manage to duck to avoid the blow (turn to **384**). If you are Unlucky, the cudgel lands heavily on the back of your head, knocking you unconscious (turn to **134**).

248

You ask Ben Borryman if he has any silver arrows for sale. He replies that he does not, but will make one for you at a cost of 10 Gold Pieces or two magic items. If you can afford his asking price, turn to **85**. If you cannot afford to pay the price, turn to **42**.

249

The Serpent Queen's head darts about you very quickly as she tries to bite you with her poisonous fangs. She will be difficult to defeat.

SERPENT QUEEN	SKILL 9	STAMINA 7

If you win, turn to **295**.

250

A small bell rings as the door opens and a creature wearing a brown apron over his clothing hurries through the archway from the back room into the shop to stand behind the counter. He appears human-like but has very ugly facial features and pointed teeth. You realize he is a crossbreed, half man, half orc. A sharp hand-axe hangs from his belt to remind you that Port Blacksand is unlikely to be a friendly place in which to do business. Will you:

Inquire about the herbs?	Turn to **183**
Ask if the Man-Orc knows of Nicodemus?	Turn to **342**
Attack the Man-Orc?	Turn to **5**

251

One of the small people stops and looks down at you. He mistakes you for a town guard and calls out to his accomplices to run for cover. Then he points a short crossbow at you and fires a bolt. *Test your Luck*. If you are Lucky, the bolt thuds into the ground at your feet (turn to **269**). If you are Unlucky, the bolt lodges deeply in your shoulder (turn to **330**).

252

The carriage is not going to stop! Suddenly the four horses, their eyes wide with terror, are almost on top of you. You must dive to one side to avoid being run down. *Test your Luck.* If you are Lucky, you escape injury from the horses as you land in the gutter (turn to **275**). If you are Unlucky, you are trampled underfoot by one of the horses (turn to **155**).

253

The SNAKES are not very tough opponents for a person trained in the art of swordsmanship. Treat them as a single creature. However, each Attack Round that they inflict a wound on you, 4 points must be subtracted from your STAMINA score because of their poisonous bite.

SNAKES	SKILL 5	STAMINA 5

If you win, you may leave the house by the front door (turn to **75**).

254

A horrified look spreads across the Vampire's face when she sees the clove of garlic in your hand. She retreats into a corner of the room trying to escape the pungent smell, which negates her blood-sucking powers. You back out of the room taking the key to the door with you, and lock it from the outside. You then run over to the staircase and climb the stairs to the next floor (turn to **310**).

255

The guards eye you suspiciously but let you walk on after seeing your pass. You walk on quickly north (turn to **227**).

256

The houses on the right-hand side of the street are small and weather-beaten. Old women sit outside on the front steps cleaning fish and mending fishing nets. They are large and jolly, talking to each other and frequently rolling about, bellowing with laughter. The fishermen do not appear to be at home. The street and the quayside come to an end at a great iron anchor. You turn round and walk back towards the junction. If you wish to stop to talk with the women, turn to **320**. If you wish to ignore them and walk straight back to the junction, turn to **369**.

257

If you are wearing the Ring of the Golden Eye, turn to **385**. If not, turn to **70**.

258

Stepping over the Fire Imp, you walk back to the stairs to see if its master is still in the house. You descend the stairs slowly, sword drawn. When you reach the bottom you are somewhat surprised to see a fat man, richly dressed, sitting in an ornate chair looking directly at you. He appears very relaxed, quite unperturbed by your drawn sword. Then he speaks, slowly and coldly, saying, 'For killing my

pet you shall pay with your life.' He raises his right hand in the air and from his outstretched fingers shoot ragged white bolts of lightning. If you are wearing an ivory skull around your neck, turn to **318**. If you do not have this item, turn to **47**.

259

You wipe the blood from your sword and walk to the wooden door. You try the handle, but it is locked. If you have a skeleton key, turn to **228**. Otherwise you may either pull on a cord hanging down in front of the door (turn to **4**) or attempt to charge the door open with your shoulder (turn to **365**).

260

The guards take their bribe and let you go. As you walk north you hear the angry shouts of the captured murderer behind you. You hurry on in case he tries to implicate you (turn to **222**).

261

'This city is ruled by Lord Azzur and he is a mean man. When you preside over the chaotic inhabitants of Port Blacksand you have to be mean. And he's the meanest. I should warn you that if you are found without a pass, you are as good as dead. I would get one if I were you, pretty quickly.' He then makes a sweeping gesture of the arm and you walk past him into the city (turn to **74**).

262

Wiping the foul-tasting soup from your lips with the back of your hand, you storm out of the house, leaving the crazy ladies to their argument. Once outside you set off east again (turn to **375**).

263

Despite the light from the burning lanterns on the landing, you are unable to see anything inside the room; it is completely black. If you have a golden owl, turn to **153**. If you do not, turn to **281**.

264

Before you are able to speak a word, the Ogre's voice booms out, saying, 'Somebody has stolen all my food. Will you give me some of yours?' If you wish to give the Ogre some of your food, deduct 2 from the Provisions on your *Adventure Sheet* and turn to **121**. If you wish to refuse his request, turn to **357**.

265

With your sword still dripping with the blood of the Rats you walk further along the tunnel. The ledge you are walking along is narrow and slippery, and you have to tread carefully so as not to fall into the slow-flowing sewage channel. The tunnel gradually bends round to the right and as you follow it round, the silence is suddenly shattered by the sound of running feet and a wailing scream. Coming straight at you, wild-eyed, with flailing arms and contorted face, uttering demon sorcery, is a white-haired old woman dressed in rags. She is a Hag. Do you possess a Potion of Mind Control? If you have this item, turn to **82**. If you do not, turn to **390**.

266

The Bays on your side are angry with you for losing the match. Some of their supporters rush over and start to jostle you. By the time you manage to drag yourself over to the wall, everyone in the arena seems to have pushed you around. Lose two items from your backpack. Eventually you climb back over the wall and walk to the junction to head west along Harbour Street (turn to **91**).

267

The two guards holding you look at each other and then at the other guard for a decision. He nods at them and they release their grip on you. As you pay him the 10 Gold Pieces he gives you a piercing look, saying, 'If Lord Azzur finds out that you are in the city without a pass, you're as good as dead. And as

for Nicodemus, find him yourself.' Suppressing an urge to draw your sword, you turn and walk into the city. Turn to 74.

268

The silk curtains in front of the archway are pulled aside and a strange creature steps into the room. It has a snake's head, which sits oddly on the shoulders of a young woman wearing a lavish gown. Its mouth opens and a forked tongue darts in and out as the Serpent Queen starts to accuse you, shouting, 'I ordered no flowers from Mrs Pipe, and she certainly would not send any as a gift. What trickery is this, rogue?' You start to panic, deciding what to do next. If you wish to run to the front door, turn to **32**. If you wish to draw your sword to attack the Serpent Queen, turn to **249**.

269

The little man with the crossbow curses before running into the building on your left. There does not appear to be an easy way to catch him, so you walk under the bridge and continue east (turn to **30**).

270

As you draw your sword the innkeeper lets out a loud whistle. A trap-door behind the bar flies open and you hear low grunting. An ugly head pops up through the door and you watch as the large green body of a TROLL emerges from a cellar. He is carrying a wooden club. The innkeeper points at you and the Troll lumbers slowly round the bar swinging his club in the air. All the tavern's customers start to chant, 'Fight! Fight! Fight!' and stand up to form a ring round you and the Troll. You are forced to fight.

TROLL	SKILL 8	STAMINA 8

If you manage to kill the Troll, turn to **26**.

271

Asleep in their bunks are three pirates. Their room is small and contains only clothing and a few personal possessions. It looks as if the pirates have been drinking and gambling – there is an uncorked bottle of rum, a mug and a pack of cards on top of a barrel in the centre of the room. You see that one of the pirates is wearing a small leather pouch around his neck. If you wish to creep up and try to cut it loose, turn to **162**. If you would rather close the door again, and not take any risks, turn to **284**.

272

You manage to squeeze yourself between the dead Centipede and the roof of the tunnel. You walk further down the tunnel and see that it ends at an iron grill through which the sewage water runs. If you wish to try to remove the grill, turn to **377**. If you wish to walk back to the entrance hole, turn to **174**.

273

Inspecting the scorpion you see that it is a brooch. You decide to pin it to your leather tunic. It is a lucky charm. Add 2 LUCK points to your total. What will you do next? You may, if you have not already done so, pick up the silver scorpion (turn to **13**). If you would rather ignore it, you may either climb the stairs (turn to **80**), or leave the house and head north (turn to **334**).

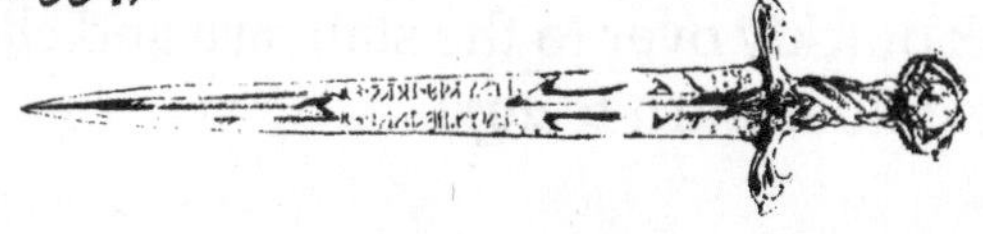

274

The guards are pleased that you have caught their wanted man. They tell you that he is an escaped murderer. The chief guard hands you 5 Gold Pieces, saying, 'Here's your reward. But you won't be getting another one – he won't escape again.' You watch for a short while as they lead the shouting murderer away, before continuing north along Stable Street (turn to **222**).

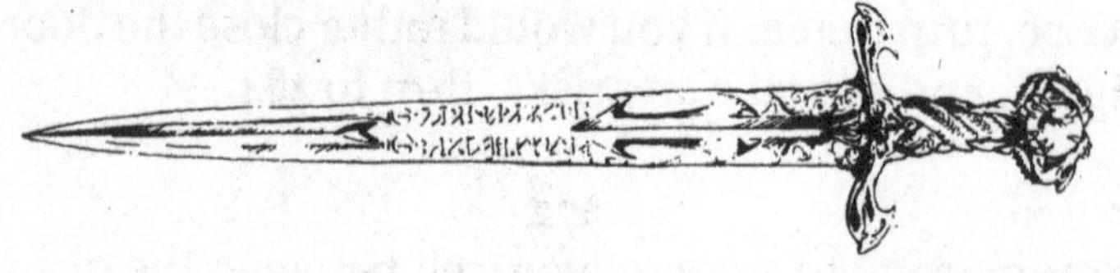

275

You stand up and brush yourself down, thinking that you would like to meet this Lord Azzur another day. The carriage races out of view and you set off west again (turn to **171**).

276

You tell the guards that you will make it worth their while if they release you and allow you entry into the city. How much will you offer them?

Five Gold Pieces?	Turn to **109**
Ten Gold Pieces?	Turn to **267**
Fifteen Gold Pieces?	Turn to **41**

277

You walk quickly over to the staircase and climb up to the next floor (turn to **207**).

278

Although many of the items in the room are extremely valuable, they are not of much use to you on your quest. However, something strange catches your eye. On a mahogany card table lie three upturned silver goblets. One is inscribed with the letter A, another with B and another with C. Will you:

Pick up goblet A?	Turn to **175**
Pick up goblet B?	Turn to **209**
Pick up goblet C?	Turn to **43**
Walk through the archway?	Turn to **107**
Climb the stairs?	Turn to **60**

279

He takes the money and motions you to sit down on a wooden stool. After a long and painful process of repeatedly pricking your forehead with a sharp needle he applies the indelible inks. You look in a mirror on the wall and find your new appearance somewhat strange. You shrug your shoulders and leave the shop; you then walk back up the lane and turn left into Mill Street (turn to **307**).

280

Further along the street on the left is another shop. A sign outside reads 'Ben Borryman, Silversmith'. If you wish to enter the shop, turn to **213**. If you would rather keep going east, turn to **100**.

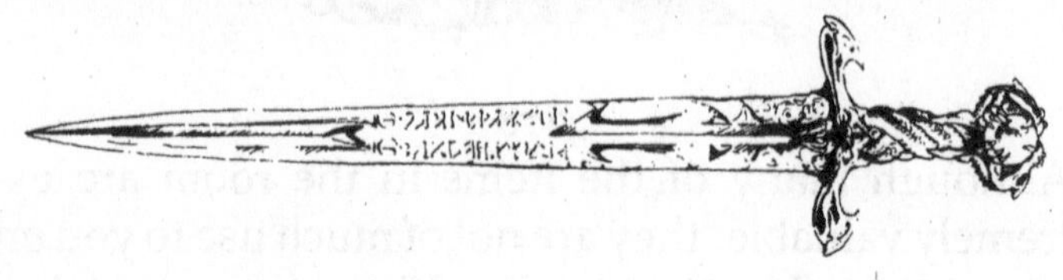

281

If you wish to grope your way into the room, turn to **391**. If you wish to walk back to the staircase to climb to the next floor, turn to **65**.

282

On the right-hand side of the street you see a large wooden barrel and a small boy sitting beside it on a stool. If you wish to talk to the boy, turn to **119**. If you wish to keep walking north, turn to **247**.

283

There is nothing useful to be found on the dead creature, so you decide to press on northwards (turn to **217**).

284

If you have not done so already, you may either open the other door (turn to **232**) or leave the ship to continue your search of Port Blacksand, walking north up Harbour Street (turn to **78**).

285

You make a rapid search through the guards' possessions and find 7 Gold Pieces, a set of keys and a piece of stale bread. Make a note of what you wish to keep and set off north again (turn to **227**).

286

You point the ring at the advancing Mummy and rub the jewel. A jet of fire flies out of the ring and the Mummy is consumed by flames. It drops to the floor and in a few moments there is nothing left but a few charred fragments. Turn to **163**.

287

The food stalls are selling fruit, vegetables, meat and hot soup, corn and chestnuts for hungry shoppers. You may eat some hot food if you wish. Pay 1 Gold Piece and increase your STAMINA by 2 points. Walking north along the west side of the square you see a man dressed in purple velvet playing a lyre. If you wish to stop and listen, turn to **3**. If you would rather walk past him, turn to **398**.

288

Nobody spends a night asleep at Zanbar Bone's tower and lives. In the middle of the night a jet of gas, which poisons you almost immediately, is released from the headboard on the bed. Then Zanbar Bone's witches and servants raise you into an undead world in which you will serve for ever as a Spirit Stalker.

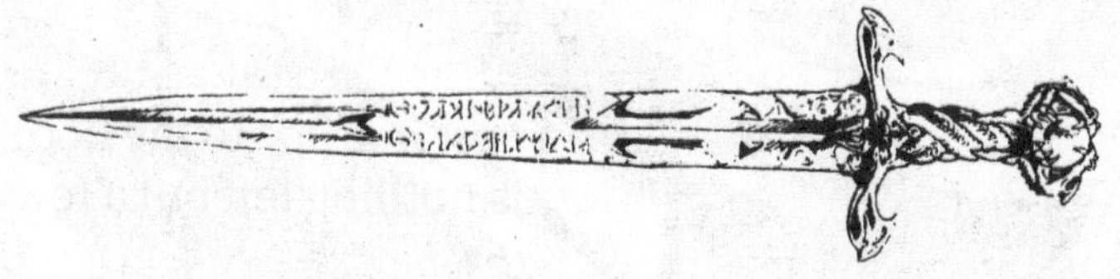

289

The Man-Orc takes your Gold Piece and spins it in the air with a flick of the thumb, catching it in the pocket of his apron. He then starts to pick his teeth with a sharpened twig and finally says, 'I know nothing about him.' If you wish to fight the impudent Man-Orc, turn to **5**. If you would rather contain your anger, leave the shop and head north again, turn to **93**.

290

You try to walk nonchalantly past the Trolls, but they suspect something odd about you and call you over to them. They ask you where you live and you reply that you are in Port Blacksand on a trading mission. The Trolls laugh scornfully and ask to see your pass. If you have a merchant's pass, turn to **219**. If you do not, turn to **335**.

291

As the guard realizes what you are doing he thrusts his pike at you. *Test your Luck.* If you are Lucky, he misses and you are able to run past him into the city (turn to **74**). If you are Unlucky, the pike pierces your arm. Lose **2** STAMINA points and turn to **10**.

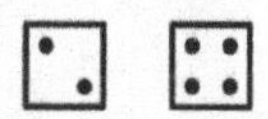

292

You walk into a lavishly furnished room containing *objets d'art* and curios. Standing before you is a young woman dressed in a black silk gown. She has long black hair and bright red lips. She smiles and motions you to sit down in one of the armchairs. You refuse to sit down, only too aware that she is one of Zanbar Bone's servants. She walks towards you open-armed as though she is about to embrace you, and when she smiles again, you see two fang-like teeth which can only belong to a Vampire. If you have some garlic, turn to **254**. If you do not have any garlic, turn to **210**.

293

She explains that she has just picked one of her golden flowers. There are ten golden petals on the flower, and you are told that if dipped in dog's blood, each petal, plucked and thrown on the ground, will change into a Gold Piece. Mrs Pipe asks for any magic item, piece of armour or food (two portions of your Provisions) in exchange for the golden flower. If you wish to trade with Mrs Pipe, make the necessary changes to your *Adventure Sheet*. Whether you trade or not, you then leave the shop and head west (turn to **24**).

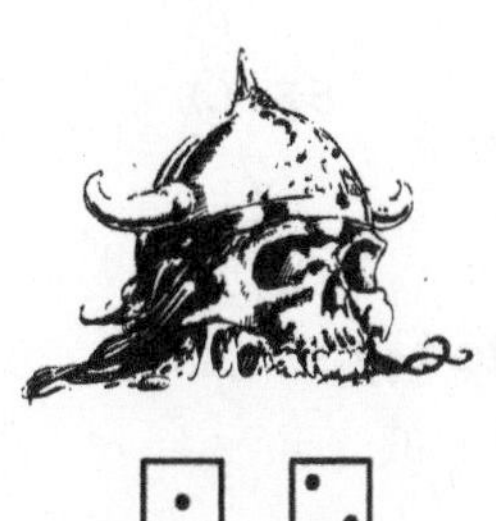

⚀ ⚁

294

At the top of the gangplank stands one of the ship's crew. On seeing you he draws his cutlass and tells you to get off the ship. If you wish to walk back down the gangplank, along the jetty and turn left up Harbour Street, turn to **78**. If you wish to draw your sword to deal with this pirate, turn to **386**.

295

You sheathe your sword and start to search the Serpent Queen's house. You find a brown leather bag which you pick up and shake. The contents make a jingling sound. Inside you find 12 Gold Pieces. Add 1 LUCK point. You leave the house and continue your walk along Stable Street (turn to **333**).

296

Walking towards you down the street are two men wearing black robes which cover them completely except for their eyes. On seeing you they nod at each other and draw their swords; they are THIEVES hoping to rob you of your possessions and you must defend yourself. Fight them one at a time.

	SKILL	STAMINA
First THIEF	7	7
Second THIEF	8	6

If you win, turn to **147**.

297

There is nothing of use to you in the room. The smell of the Zombies and the debris is terrible, so you decide to leave immediately. You walk back to the staircase to climb up to the next floor (turn to **207**).

298

You feel the effects of poison creeping through your body. Lose 4 STAMINA points. If you are still alive you manage to reach the door to escape (turn to 75).

299

It would be extremely dangerous for you to enter Port Blacksand again, especially as many of the town guards would recognize you. There is nothing else you can do but to make the long walk back to Silverton to report that you have failed in your mission.

300

The street makes a sudden right turn and heads north. You pass a cluster of small houses and are aware of unseen people watching you walk by. Then the door to one of the houses opens and a small boy dressed in rags runs out and hands you a piece of paper. Without stopping, he runs off and disappears round the corner. The paper has a message on it which reads 'Arrows from six bows are pointed at you. Leave 10 Gold Pieces in the middle of the street and keep walking.' If you want to obey the instruction, make the necessary deduction on

your *Adventure Sheet*, lose 2 LUCK points and turn to **347**. If you want to keep walking without leaving the gold, turn to **137**.

301

There is a battle-axe held in the iron-plated glove of the armour. If you wish to take the battle-axe, turn to **214**. If you wish to push the suit of armour on to the floor to make sure it is not a booby-trap, turn to **185**.

302

You show the man the two gems. Holding them up to the light he examines them carefully with a small magnifying glass. He turns to face you and offers you 9 Gold Pieces for the two. If you wish to accept the offer, turn to **240**. If you wish to haggle for a better deal, turn to **345**.

303

You bend over the motionless body of the dead Hag and you cut off a tuft of her hair with your sword. You put the hair safely in your backpack and walk back down the tunnel to the entrance hole (turn to **104**).

304

You arrive at a four-way junction in the street. The street leading west is called Key Street and the street leading east is called Clock Street. Ahead you see that Market Street continues north and a crowd of people are walking up it cheering loudly and waving their arms in the air. You decide to follow them (turn to **148**).

305

You point the mirror at the Spirit Stalker, but it does not stop him advancing. Again he manages to touch your flesh and burn you. Lose 2 STAMINA points. If you are still alive, you may either fire your silver arrow at him (turn to **189**) or fire your Ring of Ice at him (turn to **382**).

306

The two guards look at each other in horror and run out of the cell up the stairs, screaming 'Plague!' at the top of their voices. Smiling to yourself you walk calmly out of the cell and pick up your sword off the table. Upstairs you find that the guards have fled; a search of the room reveals 2 Gold Pieces and a merchant's pass to trade in Port Blacksand. Taking your findings, you move over to the door and creep outside into the city (turn to **74**).

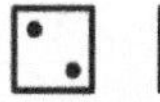

307

Walking towards you along the street are two huge guards wearing the black uniform of Lord Azzur. As they get closer you see that they are Trolls, brutal mercenaries employed by Lord Azzur as Imperial Elite Guards. To your right there is a tree which reaches almost to the top of the city wall. If you wish to risk walking past the Trolls, turn to **290**. If you wish to climb the tree in order to get over the wall, turn to **11**.

308

There is nothing to be found in the alleyway so you return to Harbour Street and turn left (turn to **180**).

309

You shake the WOLF off your arm and draw your sword. The wolf snarls and leaps at you again.

WOLF	SKILL 5	STAMINA 5

If you win, turn to **97**.

310

You climb up to the third floor and see another door at the end of the landing. If you wish to open the door, turn to **263**. If you wish to climb to the next floor, turn to **65**.

311

As you start your fight with the GUARD, you see two more armed men appear from a stone guard-house by the gate. They draw their swords and await the outcome of your battle.

CITY GUARD	SKILL 8	STAMINA 7

If you defeat the first city guard, you must now fight the other two as a pair. Both will have a separate attack on you in each Attack Round, but you must choose which of the two you will fight. Attack your nominated target as in a normal battle. Against the other you will throw for your Attack Strength in the normal way, but you will not wound him if your Attack Strength is greater – you must just count this as though you have parried his blow. Of course if his Attack Strength is greater, he will have wounded you in the normal way.

	SKILL	STAMINA
CITY GUARD	6	6
CITY GUARD	7	5

If you win, turn to **74**.

312

You notice that the Ape Man's left hand is curled into a fist. You prise open the fingers and find a tiny gold trinket in the shape of an owl. It is a magic talisman which will allow you to see in the dark. You place the owl carefully in your pocket and continue your journey (turn to **217**).

313

You retrieve your sword from the dead man's chest and hurry out of the house. Relieved to be in the open air again you set off north (turn to **304**).

314

You sit down to rest and plan what to do next. As you slump down on the cold stone floor, you inadvertently knock over a glass jar you hadn't seen before, which rolls against the wall and shatters. From the broken jar a small man some fifteen centimetres high steps out and walks over to you. He looks up at you with his hands on his hips and in a barely audible voice says, 'Thank you very much. I've been trapped in that infernal jar for the last hundred years. Now how can I repay you?' If you want to ask the whereabouts of Zanbar Bone turn to **234**. If you wish to ask if he can heal some of your wounds, turn to **94**.

315

The creature leads you downstairs to the room below and asks if you require fortune or good health. It takes the gold and silver scorpions out of their bowls and tells you that they are magic brooches. Each costs 6 Gold Pieces but you may only buy one. If you wish fortune, turn to **8**. If you wish good health, turn to **132**.

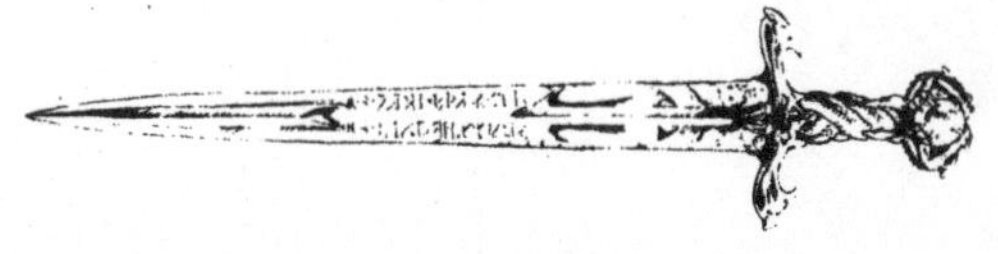

316

Once again you walk into the tattooist's shop and are greeted by Jimmy Quicktint. He is obviously pleased that you are back to give him some business (turn to **279**).

317

One of the shops to your left is a candle-maker's. There are many different coloured candles burning brightly in the window. If you wish to enter the shop, turn to **241**. If you wish to continue east, turn to **280**.

318

The skull somehow attracts and absorbs all the power of the lightning bolt, leaving you unharmed. The fat man is angry but powerless and you are able to leave the house by the front door. Once outside you set off north again (turn to **304**).

319

You enter a room which is dark and very cold. The walls and floor are made of rough stone and the room is empty except for a decorated sarcophagus. There is a strong musty smell in the air. If you want to open the sarcophagus, turn to **352**. If you wish to walk outside again, turn to **231**.

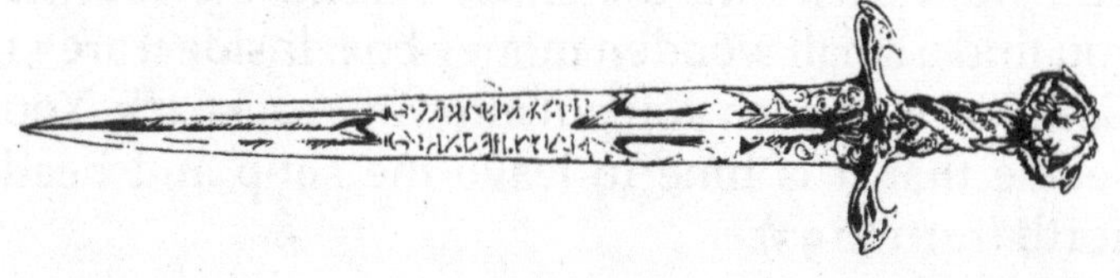

320

The jolly fishwives' plump cheeks are as round and shiny as red apples. You ask if they own any of the items you need, but they all frown and shake their heads together. Then one tells you that there is a tale that Hags have been seen disappearing down sewers to catch rats for their stew-pots. However, she has never seen a Hag herself. You decide to leave the ladies; you then walk back to the junction and turn left into Clog Street (turn to **216**).

321

At the bottom of the ladder you realize, much to your disgust, that you are standing in a sewer. There are torches along the tunnel wall, giving a very dim light, and droplets of water make eerie sounds as they fall into the sewage water. If you wish to walk north along the tunnel, turn to **356**. If you wish to walk south, turn to **118**.

322

You walk back into the shop; behind the counter you find a small wooden money box. Inside it are 11 Gold Pieces, which you put into your backpack. You decide that it is time to leave the shop and head north (turn to **93**).

323

The blacksmith looks surprised at your unprovoked aggression and pulls another red-hot iron bar from the fire with his gloved hand. He is very angry and lunges at you with the bar.

BLACKSMITH SKILL 9 STAMINA 9

If the blacksmith wounds you during any Attack Round, you must subtract 3 points from your STAMINA score because of the burn caused by the iron bar. If you win, turn to **395**.

324

The box shatters and you see two gems, 15 Gold Pieces and a white silk glove lying amidst the broken pieces of wood. If you wish to try on the glove, turn to **89**. If you wish to leave the house, taking only the gems and the gold, and continue north, turn to **282**.

325

You follow the old man through the swinging doors of the Hog and Frog tavern. He tells you to sit down at a small table in a corner while he shuffles over to the bar to buy the drinks. There are several shifty-looking characters sitting at nearby tables but they do not seem interested in you. Soon the old man comes back to the table carrying two wooden mugs

filled to the brim with cider. Once seated, he opens his leather bag and places two small pots on the table. He opens one and rubs the white cream in the pot on his wounds. He smiles and tells you that he is a chemist by trade and that you should rub some of the cream on your wounds too. You take his advice and are surprised to feel the healing effect of the cream work quickly. Add 5 STAMINA points. After finishing your drink, you say goodbye to the chemist, leave the tavern and head north (turn to 348).

326

Ahead the alleyway is strewn with rubbish and discarded possessions. Suddenly you hear growling and you see movement amongst the rubbish. You draw your sword just in time as two WILD DOGS, each a metre and a half long, leap at you. Fight both dogs at the same time.

	SKILL	STAMINA
First WILD DOG	4	4
Second WILD DOG	4	3

Both dogs will make a separate attack on you in each Attack Round, but you must choose which of the two you will fight. Attack your chosen dog as in a normal battle. Against the other you will throw for your Attack Strength in the normal way, but you will not wound it if your Attack Strength is greater; you must just count this as though you have defended yourself against its bite. Of course if its Attack Strength is greater, it will wound you. If you win, turn to **184**. You may *Escape* by running back up the alleyway and turning west into Harbour Street (turn to **180**).

327

You feel like a pincushion and although the pain is almost unbearable, you manage to stagger on down the street. Ahead to your right you see the door of one of the houses opening and a little girl looking out apprehensively. She beckons you to enter the house. If you wish to enter the house, turn to **126**. If you wish to continue walking north, turn to **164**.

328

You take the silver item out of your backpack and hand it to the Serpent Queen. She is delighted and thanks you for delivering it to her. She shows you to the front door and tips you 2 Gold Pieces. Outside you set off north along Stable Street (turn to **333**).

329

The smell by the water's edge is terrible. Above, you hear the sound of footsteps crossing the wooden bridge. Built into the foundations of the bridge is a wooden hut. Drawn curtains obstruct your view into the hut but you know you are not welcome when you read the words 'Keep Out' painted on the door in large red letters. You draw in a deep breath and knock on the door. You hear muttering and the shuffling of feet and suddenly the door is thrown open. Before you stands a white-haired old man with a long beard, wearing long white robes. He looks at you sternly and says, 'Explain yourself to Nicodemus.' You are elated at finding Nicodemus and tell him about Zanbar Bone's reign of terror in the town of Silverton and why Owen Carralif asked you to find his old friend to help them. Nicodemus frowns and walks back inside his hut, telling you to follow him. He sits down in a rocking chair and starts to speak in a calm voice. 'I am old and tired and wish for no more adventure. I live here under Singing Bridge in Port Blacksand to escape the pleas for aid from people fallen on hard times. Hence no one bothers me. But I do wish to help my old friend Owen. I will tell *you* how to defeat the Night Prince, Zanbar Bone. Listen carefully. Remember, you may defeat him only after sunset. In daylight hours he exists on another plane. No doubt he will have his servants to protect him, but should you get past them, you will need something special to deal with Bone himself. To protect yourself from his entrancing stare, you must

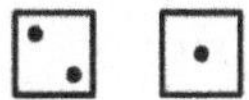

have a white unicorn in a yellow sun tattooed on your forehead. Normal weapons will not harm him. First, you must shoot him through the heart with a silver arrow. This will paralyse him but not kill him. Then you must quickly rub the ground compound of black pearl, Hag's hair and a lotus flower in his open eyes. With luck, he will decay before you in seconds. If your arrow misses, I'm afraid you will die the moment he touches you. The items for the compound can all be found in Port Blacksand if you search hard enough. I regret I cannot accompany you.' Nicodemus then draws you a map of how to reach Zanbar Bone's guarded tower from Port Blacksand. He stands up, shakes your hand and wishes you well. You leave his hut, climb the steps and cross the bridge over Catfish River. Bridge Street continues north a short distance before ending at a junction. If you wish to walk west down Harbour Street, turn to **91**. If you wish to turn east down Candle Street, turn to **238**.

330

Lose 3 STAMINA points. If you are still alive you manage with great pain to pull the bolt from your shoulder. As you bandage your wound the little man runs off into the building on your left. There does not appear to be an easy way to catch him so you walk under the bridge and continue east (turn to **30**).

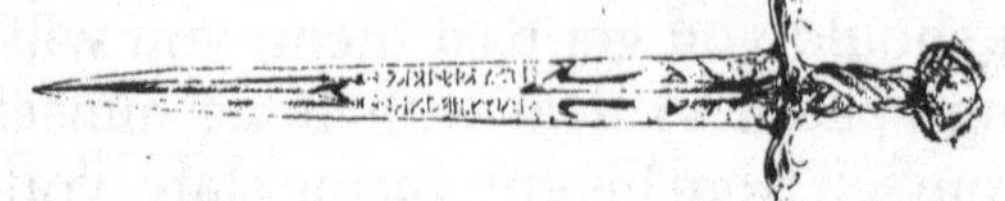

331

As you approach the man, he suddenly springs up and screams at the top of his voice. He produces a dagger from his ragged clothing and leaps at you. His wild eyes belong to a man insane or possessed and you must fight him.

MAD MAN	SKILL 5	STAMINA 5

If you win, turn to **86**.

332

The beggar tips his hat in gratitude and mumbles a few words. Add 1 LUCK point before continuing west (turn to **124**).

333

You soon reach a junction in the street. Stable Street continues north and to your left you see Tower Street leading west. You decide to keep going north (turn to **76**).

334

Walking towards you down the street are two town guards. They stop in front of you and demand to see your papers. If you possess a merchant's pass, turn to **255**. If you do not, turn to **99**.

335

The larger of the two Trolls tells you that you are under arrest for being in Port Blacksand without authorization. He tells you that he is feeling generous, however, and offers you a choice. You can pay a fine of all the gold in your backpack and be thrown out of the city, or spend a year with rats and cockroaches in a dirty dungeon cell. The other Troll bursts out laughing, saying, 'Generous? Ho! Ho! Ho! Ah, Sourbelly, you've got such a sense of humour!' If you wish to pay the fine and be thrown out of the city, turn to **367**. If you wish to resist arrest, turn to **73**.

336

Once inside the shop you realize why the windows are barred – it is a jeweller's shop. Standing behind the glass counter is a huge bald-headed man with an eye-patch covering his left eye. He gives you a welcoming smile but the sight of his ugly mouth with its few black-stained teeth does not inspire confidence. A large battle-axe hangs conveniently behind the man to deter any would-be robbers. On display are several ornate rings inset with diamonds, emeralds and rubies. The man asks whether you are buying or selling. Will you:

Ask the price of the rings?	Turn to **36**
Offer to sell him gems (if you have them)?	Turn to **302**
Attack him with your sword?	Turn to **170**

337

Congratulations – you have killed Zanbar Bone, the infamous Night Prince. He decays before your eyes, becoming nothing more than a small pile of powder on the floor (turn to **400**).

338

You have just swallowed a Potion of Misfortune. Reduce your LUCK by 3 points. Hoping for better luck ahead you set off north again (turn to **105**).

339

The man looks at you and smiles, saying, 'We do not get many visitors in these parts, but I am sure my master would wish you to have a room for the night. Do come in.' He steps back and you follow him into a beautiful marble-floored hallway. There are portraits and shields hanging on the walls and a spiral staircase leads up to the floor above. He asks you to follow him up the staircase and offers to carry your backpack for you, which you allow him to do. You can see that the staircase winds its way all the way up to the top of the tower, but the man steps off at the first floor and walks along the landing to a door. He opens it and walks into a large room, placing your backpack on a made-up bed. He tells you that this is your room for the night and walks out, telling

you that you will meet his master at breakfast. If you wish to lock the door and go to bed, turn to **288**. If you wish to explore the tower after waiting a few minutes, turn to **77**.

340

Once more you poke the wire inside the lock and finally it turns. Add 1 LUCK point. Raising the lid of the chest you see, to your delight, 25 Gold Pieces and a magnificent shield. If you use this shield in battle, it will increase your Attack Strength by 1 during each Attack Round. You may now either climb the stairs to the floor above (turn to **60**) or leave the house to head north (turn to **304**).

341

You decide that you are going to have to make a run for it or risk being put in jail. You take 5 Gold Pieces out of your backpack and throw them on the floor. The guards bend down to pick them up and you run north as fast as you can. As you run off, the escaped murderer starts to yell and two of the guards chase after you. In an alleyway to your left you see a large open barrel which you dive into. You hear the guards run past but you wait a few minutes before climbing out of the barrel. You look up and down Stable Street and all is clear. Once more you set off north (turn to **222**).

342

The Man-Orc tells you that for 1 Gold Piece he will tell you all he knows. If you want to pay for his information, turn to **289**. If you would rather leave the shop and continue your walk north, turn to **93**.

343

You fall to the floor, unconscious. Lose 3 STAMINA points. If you are still alive, you awake to find yourself lying outside the shop in Clog Street. You will find that any silver items you had are now missing. You stand up and set off angrily along the street (turn to **100**).

344

You step out into the middle of the street and wait. Suddenly a pair of horses come galloping into view pulling an ornate gold carriage. The driver sees you and, cracking his whip, yells, 'Make way for Lord Azzur!' If you wish to step out of the path of the oncoming carriage, turn to **58**. If you wish to stay where you are, turn to **252**.

345

The man frowns and thumps his fist down on top of the counter, shouting, 'This is not a bazaar! If you do not like my prices, take your custom elsewhere. Now get out of my shop before I slice you in two.' Will you:

Calm him down and accept his offer?	Turn to **240**
Walk out of the shop and head west?	Turn to **196**
Attack him with your sword?	Turn to **170**

346

The distance to the ground is too great even for a great warrior like yourself. You land badly and break your neck. Your adventure ends here.

347

You hurry on down the street but glance back after hearing cries of jubilation behind you. Some people are linked arm in arm and are dancing in a circle round your 10 Gold Pieces. You curse this thieving city and press on north (turn to **112**).

348

Tower Street makes a sharp turn to the right, going east between tall buildings. An iron bridge crosses overhead between two of the buildings and you see movement on it. Small cloaked people are carrying laden sacks between the buildings, apparently in a great hurry. If you wish to call out to them, turn to **251**. If you wish to walk under the bridge and continue east, turn to **30**.

349

Suddenly you are confronted by a small winged creature, no more than a metre in length, hovering before you. It is red in colour and has two horns protruding from its head and a small tail hanging down from its back. It will be difficult to defeat as it flies quickly about your head spitting fire at you!

FIRE IMP	SKILL 9	STAMINA 4

If you win, turn to **258**. You may *Escape* by jumping out of the window to the street below (turn to **192**).

350

You open your backpack and pretend to search for the flowers. The Serpent Queen starts to fidget and you can see her becoming increasingly impatient. You cannot think of a good plan and start to panic. If you wish to run to the front door, turn to **32**. If you wish to draw your sword to attack the Serpent Queen, turn to **249**.

351

You take 10 Gold Pieces out of your backpack and place them on the palm of the hand outstretched before you. The old man then reaches into his inner clothing and pulls out an iron key, telling you that it will unlock your cell. Almost in disbelief you take the key and place it in the lock. Incredibly, the lock turns. You look back at the old man and ask him if he wishes to escape with you. He smiles and shakes his head, saying that he is happy where he is. You leave the cell and, picking up your sword, climb the stairs to the floor above. The two guards are relaxing over a game of cards. You wave your sword in the air and charge at them. They grab their swords to defend themselves and fight you one at a time.

	SKILL	STAMINA
First CITY GUARD	6	6
Second CITY GUARD	7	5

If you win, turn to **54**.

352

You lift the lid of the sarcophagus and see a human body completely encased in old bandages. The light, although dim, has disturbed the sleep of a MUMMY, and it sits up, turning its head from side to side. It senses where you are and starts to climb out of its sarcophagus. It walks towards you with its arms extended. If you wish to fight the Mummy, turn to **193**. If you have a Lantern, you may throw it at the Mummy (turn to **106**).

353

You try to turn the large brass handle on the door but it is locked. If you have an iron key, turn to **181**. If you do not, you may either try to force the door open (turn to **389**) or return to the street to head north (turn to **304**).

354

The tattooist looks at you with a bored expression on his face and says, 'Well, you don't expect me to do it for free, do you? If you've got anything worth selling, go next door. My step-brother lives there and he's a pawnbroker. Tell him I sent you and maybe he'll give you a good price.' You walk outside and knock on the wooden door of the next house. A squint-eyed man opens the door and you tell him that you want to sell some items so that you can afford to have a tattoo. The man asks you to come into his house and you enter a room piled high with all kinds of objects, furniture, armour, curios and pottery. He explains that he has a stall in the market which he rents once a week. He then tells you what he is currently interested in buying, and the prices he is offering:

Silver goblet	8 Gold Pieces
Skeleton key	15 Gold Pieces
Scorpion brooch	10 Gold Pieces
Magic ring	12 Gold Pieces
Silver bracelet	5 Gold Pieces

more overleaf

Helmet	7 Gold Pieces
Silver flute	5 Gold Pieces
Eye-patch	1 Gold Piece
Knucklebones	1 Gold Piece
Mirror	1 Gold Piece

You may sell the pawnbroker any of your possessions. You bid him farewell and walk outside. If you have enough money for the price of a tattoo, turn to **316**. If you still cannot afford one, you will have to come back again later. You walk back up the lane and turn left into Mill Street (turn to **307**).

355

You turn on the two guards who were holding you and, before they realize what is happening, you smash their heads together, knocking them unconscious. You dash into the city (turn to **74**).

356

Ahead you hear the sound of squealing and frantic splashing. Long shadows are cast by moving objects coming towards you. Then you see the sleek, glistening shapes of three GIANT RATS only a few metres away from you. You draw your sword hastily and fight each of the Rats in turn.

	SKILL	STAMINA
First RAT	4	4
Second RAT	5	4
Third RAT	5	5

If you win, turn to **28**.

357

The OGRE is mad with hunger and picks up a large bone off the floor. He raises it above his head and lumbers towards you. You must fight him.

OGRE	SKILL 8	STAMINA 9

If you defeat him, turn to **71**. After the third Attack Round, you may *Escape* by running out of the house and heading north (turn to **282**).

358

It's a close shave, but you just manage to grip the edge of the wall with your fingertips. You pull yourself up and climb on to a stone walkway along the top of the city wall. On either side of you are stone towers rising above the battlements, spaced some hundred metres apart. There are doors in the towers, both of which are suddenly flung open as more guards run out to capture you. There is a twenty-metre drop on the other side of the wall. Will you:

Jump to freedom?	Turn to **346**
Fix a Climbing Rope (if you have one) to the wall and climb down the other side?	Turn to **108**
Face the oncoming guards?	Turn to **56**

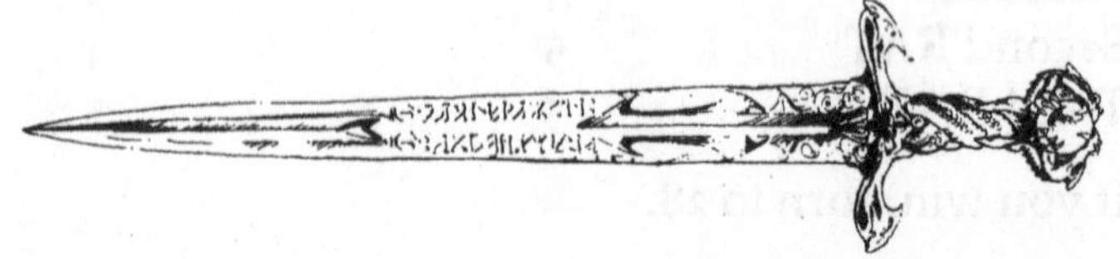

359

All the Bays on your side rush over to you and slap your hands with theirs. They are overjoyed at their victory. Supporters run over and start handing you gifts. Eventually you manage to wriggle free from your admirers and find a place to sit down to inspect your gifts. You have been given 8 Gold Pieces, a bottle containing a clear liquid labelled 'Potion of Mind Control', a silver flute, a bunch of bananas, a piece of chalk and an eye-patch. You eat the bananas (add 2 STAMINA points) and place the rest of the items in your backpack. You climb back over the wall before the Bays start another game, walk back to the junction and head west along Harbour Street (turn to **91**).

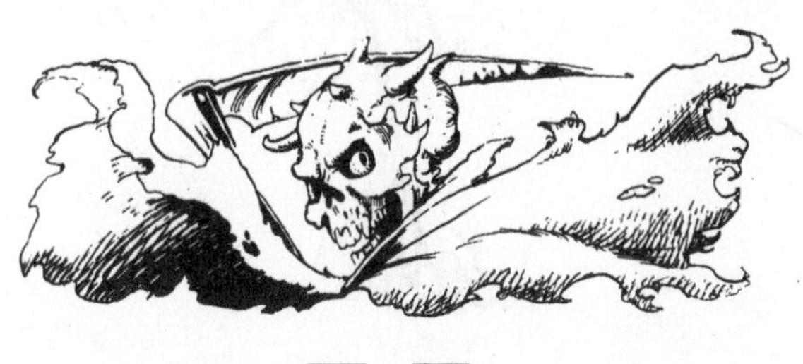

⚀ ⚂

360

During your fight with the Wolf Dogs, Wraggins runs out of the front of the shop, perhaps to fetch help. If you wish to stay and search the shop, turn to **123**. If you would rather hurry out and continue west along Key Street, turn to **300**.

361

The mindless ZOMBIES step slowly towards you with their sticks raised in the air. Fight them one at a time.

	SKILL	STAMINA
First ZOMBIE	6	6
Second ZOMBIE	6	7

If you win, turn to **297**.

362

The boots fit perfectly and walking about you feel very sure-footed. They are magic elven boots. Add 1 SKILL point to your total and set off east again (turn to **103**).

363

In the middle of the street you see a large manhole cover. If you wish to lift the manhole cover to see where it leads to, turn to **48**. If you wish to keep walking east, turn to **205**.

364

The gaunt-faced man looks thoroughly miserable. He sees you and shrinks back, telling you that it is not worth robbing him because he has no money. You tell him that you do not wish to rob him but are seeking an old wizard named Nicodemus. He stares at you with a surprised expression on his face and says, 'For 2 Gold Pieces, I'll tell you where he is.' You decide to trust the man and pay him for his information. He pockets the gold and says, 'You are standing on top of him! Nicodemus lives in a hut underneath this bridge.' He throws back his head and lets out a shrill laugh before hobbling off on his crutches, obviously pleased with himself. You shake your head and walk over to the steps that lead down beneath the bridge (turn to **329**).

365

You charge the door several times before it splinters. Unfortunately, you injure your shoulder in the process. Lose 1 SKILL point. Through the broken door you see a thin, pale-skinned man with dark, hollow eyes, wearing a servant's uniform. In a cold, hissing voice he says, 'Really, do you have to make such a dramatic entry? Could you not have pulled the bell cord like everybody else?' If you wish to apologize and tell him that you are a lost traveller, turn to **339**. If you wish to attack him with your sword, turn to **35**.

366

You pay for the smoking mixture and leave the shop. Outside you pack your pipe with the smoking mixture and light it. The smoke is dark and tastes awful. You start to cough and your chest is gripped by a terrible pain. Lose 2 STAMINA points. You are unable to stop coughing, so you sit down on the street and try to calm down. You slump down against a wall between two barrels and gradually the coughing subsides. If you want to go back to the herbalist to complain, turn to **101**. If you would rather walk north again, turn to **93**.

367

The Trolls watch carefully as you open your backpack. You give them all your gold except for 1 Gold Piece which you manage to palm without their noticing. They then place themselves on either side of you and march you along Mill Street until you reach the city's North Gate at the junction with Goose Street. They tell the two guards on duty not to let you back into Port Blacksand. They give you a forceful boot up the backside and you land sprawling on the dusty road outside. Do you have all the items required to slay the Night Prince, and have you been tattooed? If you have, turn to **201**. If you are missing any of the items, or have not been tattooed, turn to **299**.

368

Looking into a crystal ball, she seems to go into a trance. She tells you that you are searching for a man, a wise man with magical powers. She pauses for a moment and then draws in a deep breath before going on to tell you that the man you are looking for lives in a hut beneath a bridge to the north. She warns you to be careful when approaching the man, for he does not welcome strangers. Then she looks away from the crystal ball and asks you to leave. Her face seems to be hiding something. Has she seen some dreadful fate awaiting you? You decide to leave the tent and head north (turn to **117**).

369

Back at the junction you turn left into Clog Street and walk eastwards (turn to **216**).

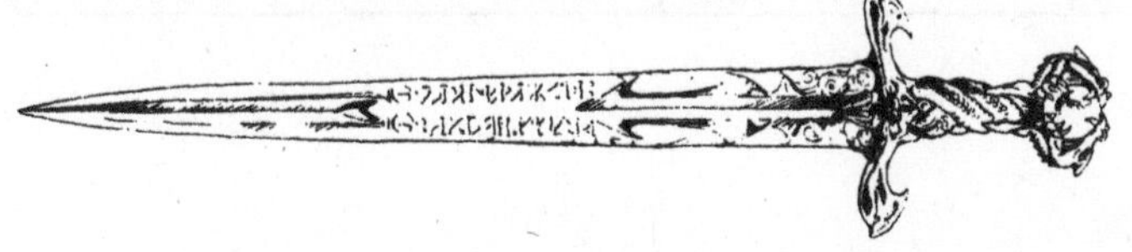

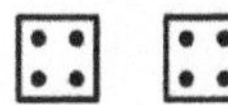

DO NOT
Pick
Flowers

370

You place the coin in the slot and walk through the turnstile. Although the flowers and shrubs are not outstanding, you are nevertheless surprised that such a place exists in Port Blacksand. The gardens are not very large, extending back some sixty metres to where some houses back on to them. There are two paths to follow, one of which runs around the edge of the gardens and one that leads directly into the centre, where there is some topiary – each shrub has been cut into the shape of an animal – and you decide to take a closer look. The path leads into a small paved area surrounded by the animal-shaped shrubs. In the middle there is a stone plinth upon which sits a large earthen bowl containing lotus flowers! There is a painted sign which reads 'Do Not Pick the Flowers'. The gardener is nowhere to be seen and there is nobody else about. If you wish to risk picking one of the flowers, turn to **14**. If you would rather leave the gardens and continue north, turn to **133**.

371

In the back room of the shop you find a glass jar on a dusty shelf labelled 'Healing Mixture'. If you wish to apply some of it to your wounds (if you suffered any), turn to **83**. If you would rather continue searching the shop, turn to **322**.

372

The houses in this section of Stable Street consist of two rows of terraces. They are all made of sandstone

apart from one in the middle of the terrace to your right, which is made of brick and is painted white. The door is made of oak and a serpent's head is carved into it. If you wish to enter the white house, turn to **131**. If you wish to keep walking north, turn to **333**.

373

You grimace as you feel the poison creep up your arm. Lose 4 STAMINA points and 1 SKILL point. If you are still alive, you may (if you have not done so already) lift goblet B (turn to **209**) or goblet C (turn to **43**). If you have lost interest in the goblets, you may either walk through the archway (turn to **107**) or climb the stairs (turn to **60**).

374

The shield was taken from a goodly knight who died at the hand of Zanbar Bone. It was forged with good magic. Add 1 SKILL point. You walk over to the spiral staircase with your new shield and climb to the floor above (turn to **21**).

375

Eventually the street comes to a dead end at a high stone wall. There are stone steps leading to the top of the wall. On the other side of the wall you can hear grunts, growls and cheering. If you wish to climb over the wall, turn to **40**. If you wish to walk back to the junction and head west down Harbour Street, turn to **91**.

376

The helmet fits on your head perfectly, as though it had been specially made for you. It has magic properties also, and will allow you to add 1 point to all future dice rolls when computing your Attack Strength during combat as long as you wear it – add 1 LUCK point. You set off east again (turn to **161**).

377

The iron grill is securely bolted to the brick wall and you are unable to remove it. However, above the grill you notice a dark recess where some bricks have been removed from the wall. It is too dark to see deep inside the recess. If you wish to put your hand into the dark hole, turn to **92**. If you would rather walk back to the entrance hole, turn to **174**.

378

Roll one die alternately for yourself and for the bare-chested man, to represent the cannon-ball passing between you. Repeat this process until a 1 is thrown, in which case the cannon-ball will have been dropped and the loser must pay the winner 5 Gold Pieces. After finishing the game you walk on a bit further (turn to **52**).

379

Lose 2 STAMINA points. Despite the pain in your arm you must act quickly to escape the advancing Suit of Armour. If you wish to open the door in front of you, turn to **122**. If you wish to run back to the staircase to climb up to the next floor, turn to **207**.

380

Despite its rotten taste, the soup includes herbs blended in an ancient tradition which are beneficial to health. Add 4 STAMINA points. Feeling somewhat revitalized you decide to leave the ladies to their argument and head east (turn to **375**).

381

The guard frowns and says, 'A likely story, I'm sure. But I suppose you are just the same as all the rest inside this city. You may enter at your own peril or buy my advice for 3 Gold Pieces.' If you wish to head straight into the city, turn to **74**. If you wish to buy the guard's advice, make the necessary deduction on your *Adventure Sheet* and turn to **261**.

382

A jet of gas shoots out of the ring and turns to ice on contact with the Spirit Stalker, covering him completely. It does not stop him advancing towards you, but it slows him down. You have time either to fire your silver arrow at him (turn to **189**) or to reflect his stare in your mirror (turn to **305**), as your Ring of Ice is useless.

383

If you have not done so already, you may open the other door (turn to **271**) or leave the ship to continue your search of Port Blacksand, walking north up Harbour Street (turn to **78**).

384

As the cudgel swings through the air above your head, you punch the Dwarf holding it. He lets out a scream and drops the cudgel. Feeling his bleeding nose and seeing the blood on his hand, he screams again and runs off down the alley. The other two Dwarfs holding your legs realize that you are not an easy victim and run off after their fellow-robber. If you wish to chase them down the alley, turn to **221**. If you wish to set off west again, turn to **396**.

385

A voice in your mind tells you that the chest is an illusion and does not exist. Also you see that the black cat is not what you thought it was. Before you stands a black-robed skeleton with green, translucent eyes, wearing a golden crown on its skull – Zanbar Bone! Before you have time to notch your arrow, the Night Prince pulls three teeth from his mouth and throws them on to the floor. They explode in puffs of smoke and out of them step three SKELETONS armed with swords. Fight them one at a time.

	SKILL	STAMINA
First SKELETON	6	7
Second SKELETON	8	6
Third SKELETON	7	7

If you win, turn to **203**.

386

The PIRATE seems pleased that you wish to fight him and grins, revealing a toothless mouth which unnerves you a little.

PIRATE	SKILL 7	STAMINA 5

If you win, turn to **20**.

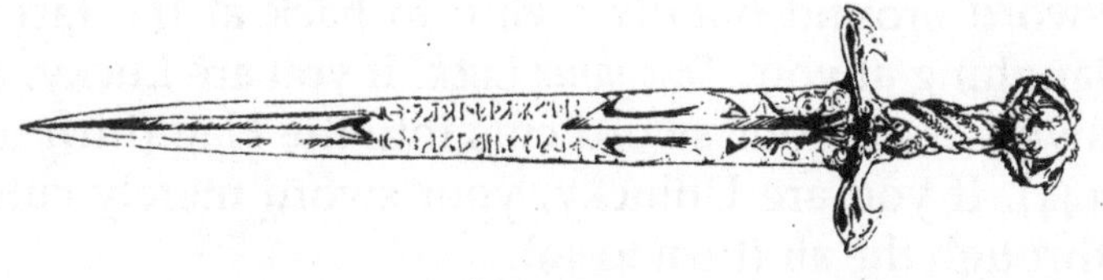

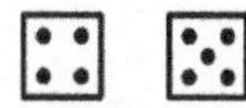

387

You are now wearing a brooch that slows you down in combat without your realizing it. Reduce your SKILL by 1 point. Finding nothing else of interest in the room you decide to go back down the stairs and leave the house to head north (turn to **334**).

388

You try with all your might to bend the bars securing the glass cupboard but you are unable to open it. Finding nothing else of interest in the shop, you walk outside and continue east (turn to **100**).

389

You push the door with your shoulder with all your might. Roll two dice. If the number rolled is less than or equal to your SKILL score, the door flies open (turn to **159**). If the number rolled is greater than your SKILL, the door remains firmly shut. You decide not to risk injury to yourself and walk back to the street, continuing northwards (turn to **304**).

390

The HAG is conjuring a spell which instils terrible fear in you. Your mind is full of illusions and you think you are being burned alive with a crowd of skeletal faces looking on gleefully. You swing your sword around blindly trying to hack at the faces laughing at you. *Test your Luck*. If you are Lucky, a swipe from your sword cuts into the Hag (turn to **144**). If you are Unlucky, your sword merely cuts through the air (turn to **59**).

391

Unbeknown to you, there is a trip-wire across the doorway at your feet and a crossbow on the wall opposite, so that as you walk into the room you trigger the wire and this releases the crossbow bolt straight at you. *Test your Luck.* If you are Lucky, you trip over the wire and fall on the floor; the crossbow bolt flies over your head and through the door (turn to **235**). If you are Unlucky, the bolt sinks into your chest (turn to **142**).

392

The creature is outraged that you have stolen one of its brooches. It jumps up and you notice smoke curling up from its nostrils as its fury mounts. Suddenly a blast of fire shoots from its jaw and it moves towards you with outstretched claws. The blast misses you but you must fight the creature.

LIZARDINE SKILL 8 STAMINA 8

As well as following the usual rules of battle, throw one die every Attack Round for the Lizardine's fiery breath. On a roll of 1, 2 or 3, it burns you for 1 point of damage to be subtracted from your STAMINA. On a roll of 4, 5 or 6 you manage to dodge the blast. You may use your LUCK against the fire and you may *Escape* by running back down the stairs and out of the house to head north (turn to **334**). If you stay and win the battle, turn to **186**.

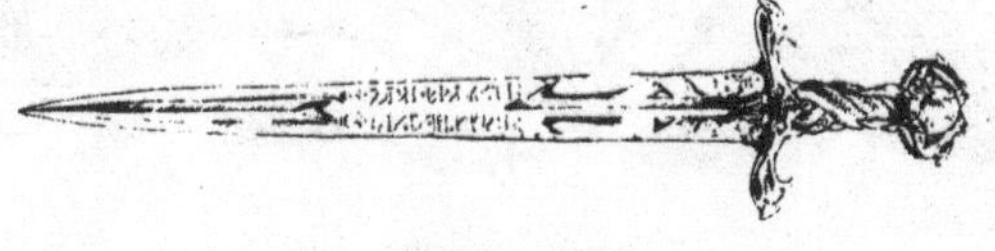

393

You tell the Trolls that you are a weapon-maker and have been to the market to sell daggers to a stall-holder there. Sourbelly sneers at you and says, 'Well in that case you have finished your business in Port Blacksand. Allow us to escort you to the city gates.' If you wish to let them throw you out of the city, turn to **156**. If you wish to attack the Trolls, turn to **73**.

394

Sitting behind a small table is a plump woman wearing bright yellow clothes and a shawl over her head. She smiles as you enter, bidding you to sit down. She tells you that a glimpse of the future will cost you 2 Gold Pieces. If you wish to pay to hear her predictions, turn to **368**. If you would rather carry on unaided, leave the tent and head north (turn to **117**).

395

The blacksmith was a good man. Lose 4 LUCK points. Feeling extremely guilty, you leave the stable and continue north (turn to **115**).

396

On the left side of the street is a flower shop. The window is filled with exotic and colourful flowers. If you wish to enter the shop, turn to **145**. If you prefer to keep walking west, turn to **24**.

397

No wonder the vagabonds wanted to rob you – they only have 1 Gold Piece between them. You find nothing else of interest in their pockets and so decide to set off north along Stable Street (turn to **372**).

398

A small circle of people is standing around a bare-chested man. He is enormous and his muscles look as hard as iron. He is asking the crowd for a volunteer to play catch with a cannon-ball. He states that whoever drops the cannon-ball must pay the other 5 Gold Pieces. If you wish to take him on at his game, turn to **378**. If you would rather walk on, turn to **52**.

399

A rope ladder hangs down from the stern of the ship to the jetty. There is also a gangplank leading up the side of the ship. If you wish to board the ship by climbing the rope ladder, turn to **87**. If you wish to walk straight up the gangplank, turn to **294**.

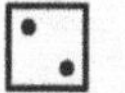 

400

You leave Zanbar Bone's black tower as quickly as you can, not wishing to spend another moment in the infernal place. Before leaving, however, you set it alight so that no evil entity may ever again use it for foul deeds. You sleep the rest of the night and long into the next morning in a hayfield, before setting off for Silverton in the afternoon. Battle-weary and hungry, you arrive in Silverton the same evening. You are given a hero's welcome and gift after gift is bestowed upon you. A feast is arranged and there is laughter, music and drinking in all the streets. Finally, Owen Carralif makes a speech and presents you with a gold orb worth hundreds of Gold Pieces. The people of Silverton are joyous once again.

CHOOSE YOUR ADVENTURER

Here at your disposal are three adventurers to choose from. Over the page are the rules for Fighting Fantasy to help you on your way. However, if you wish to begin your adventure immediately, study the characters carefully, log their attributes on the Adventure Sheet and you can begin!

Barik Shabdark

As a descendant of the ancient Celenasian aristocracy, Barik Shabdark has long had a destiny to fulfill. His ancestors from an empire now lost beneath the Plane of Bones were renowned heroes of legend and tales of their deeds are recited in the lands of Allansia and far across the sea.

Barik has travelled the length and breadth of Allansia in pursuit of fame and fortune, and has recently begun to emulate the feats of his forebears. A supremely skilled swordsman, numerous lords within the Vale of Willow's many towns have employed his skills to slay fearsome monsters, bandits and troublesome wizards. Less than a year ago Barik defeated the evil Sllarssshra, a powerful Red Dragon on the borders of the Forest of Yore in what has since become known as the 'Duelling of the Flames'.

Skill	12
Stamina	19
Luck	7
Potion	Skill
Provisions	6 Meals

Helios Wardalus

An only child, Helios Wardalus grew up as an orphan following the disappearance of his father, the famed prophet Hallan Wardalus and the banishment of his mother, the sorceress Volee Hanu.

Helios rose from obscurity after being apprenticed within the army of King Salamon LVII. Within a few years he had become the prominent embodiment of a Salamonian officer, overseeing numerous key victories against the migrating goblinoid tribes of the Giant Mounds to the south east of Salamonis.

Now departed from the Salamonis army, Helios is a strong and powerfully built strong-arm, who tends to use his large physical presence to solve any problems he encounters. This strength has come to his aid on numerous occasions, and he has used it to intimidate foes, endure dangerous conditions and complete feats few could ever hope to accomplish.

Skill	9
Stamina	23
Luck	6
Potion	Strength
Provisions	6 Meals

Tarak Kharnbak

As a refugee of the city of fallen city of Vymorna in the southern lands of Allansia, Tarak has endured the loss of her friends, her family and her home. During the siege of the Lizard Men, Tarak was second-in-command of the Coppertown garrison. Despite facing overwhelming odds and losing many brave comrades, Tarak had been blessed by the goddess Avana who ensured she always came through unscathed.

When the city eventually fell to the Silur Cha empire she was among the fortunate few to escape a mounting Serpent War, fleeing first to Wolftown before making her way in the world as a renowned adventurer.

Tarak is unusually tall and rarely recounts stories of her battles or the loss of her family, as the memories are too painful. She speaks only when spoken too and has a devout faith in the goddess Avana and the gift of good fortune bestowed upon her for reasons she fails to comprehend.

Skill	10
Stamina	16
Luck	12
Potion	Fortune
Provisions	6 Meals

HOW TO FIGHT THE CREATURES OF THE CITY OF THIEVES

Before embarking on your adventure, you must first determine your own strengths and weaknesses by rolling dice to determine your initial scores. On pages 208–209 there is an *Adventure Sheet* which you may use to record the details of an adventure. On it you will find boxes for recording your SKILL, STAMINA and LUCK scores. You are advised to either record your scores on the Adventure Sheet in pencil, or make photocopies of the sheet to use in future adventures.

Skill, Stamina and Luck

To determine your *Initial* SKILL, STAMINA and LUCK scores:

Roll one die. Add 6 to this number and enter this total in the SKILL box on the *Adventure Sheet*.

Roll both dice. Add 12 to the number rolled and enter this total in the STAMINA box.

Roll one die, add 6 to this number and enter this total in the LUCK box.

SKILL reflects your swordsmanship and fighting expertise; the higher the better. STAMINA represents your strength; the higher your STAMINA, the longer you will survive. LUCK represents how lucky a person you are. Luck – and magic – are facts of life in the fantasy world you are about to explore.

SKILL, STAMINA and LUCK scores change constantly during an adventure, so keep an eraser handy. You must keep an accurate record of these scores. But never rub out your *Initial* scores. Although you may receive additional SKILL, STAMINA and LUCK points, these totals may never exceed your *Initial* scores, except on very rare occasions, when instructed on a particular page.

Battles

When you are told to fight a creature, you must resolve the battle as described below. First record the creature's SKILL and STAMINA scores (as given on the page) in an empty *Monster Encounter Box* on your *Adventure Sheet*. The sequence of combat is then:

1. Roll the two dice for the creature. Add its SKILL score. This total is **its** *Attack Strength*.
2. Roll the two dice for yourself. Add your current SKILL. This total is **your** *Attack Strength*.
3. Whose *Attack Strength* is higher? If your *Attack Strength* is higher, you have wounded the creature. If the creature's *Attack Strength* is higher, it has wounded you. (If both are the same, you have both missed – start the next *Attack Round* from step 1 above.)
4. If you wounded the creature, subtract 2 points from **its** STAMINA score. You may use LUCK here to do additional damage (see 'Using Luck in Battles' below).

5. If the creature wounded you, subtract 2 points from **your** STAMINA score. You may use LUCK to minimize the damage (see below).
6. Make the appropriate changes to either the creature's or your own STAMINA scores (and your LUCK score if you used LUCK) and begin the next *Attack Round* (repeat steps 1–6).
7. This continues until the STAMINA score of either you or the creature you are fighting has been reduced to zero (death).

Luck

Sometimes you will be told to *Test your Luck*. As you will discover, using Luck is a risky business. The way you *Test your Luck* is as follows:

Roll two dice. If the number rolled is *equal to* or *less than* your current LUCK score, you have been *lucky*. If the number rolled is *higher* than your current LUCK score, you have been *unlucky*. The consequences of being *lucky* or *unlucky* will be found on the page. Each time you *Test your Luck*, you must subtract one point from your current LUCK score. So the more you rely on luck, the more risky this becomes.

Using Luck in Battles

In battles, you always have the option of using your luck either to score a more serious wound on a creature, or to minimize the effects of a wound the creature has just scored on you.

If you have just wounded the creature: you may *Test your Luck* as described above. If you are *lucky*, subtract an *extra* 2 points from the creature's STAMINA score (i.e. 4 instead of 2 normally). But if you are *unlucky*, you must restore 1 point to the creature's STAMINA (so instead of scoring the normal 2 points of damage, you have now scored only 1).

If the creature has just wounded you: you can *Test your Luck* to try to minimize the wound. If you are *lucky*, restore 1 point of your STAMINA (ie. instead of doing 2 points of damage, it has done only 1). If you are *unlucky*, subtract 1 *extra* STAMINA point.

Don't forget to subtract 1 point from your LUCK score each time you *Test your Luck*.

Restoring Skill, Stamina and Luck

Skill

Occasionally, a page may give instructions to alter your SKILL score. A Magic Weapon may increase your SKILL, but remember that only one weapon can be used at a time! You cannot claim 2 SKILL bonuses for carrying two Magic Swords. Your SKILL score can never exceed its *Initial* value unless specifically instructed. Drinking the Potion of Skill (see later) will restore your SKILL to its *Initial* level at any time.

Stamina and Provisions

Your STAMINA score will change a lot during the adventure. As you near your goal, your STAMINA level may be dangerously low and battles may be particularly risky, so be careful!

You start the game with enough Provisions for ten meals. A separate *Provisions Remaining* box is provided on the *Adventure Sheet* for recording details of *Provisions*. You may eat only **one** meal at a time. When you eat a meal, add 4 points to your STAMINA score and deduct 1 point from your *Provisions*. Remember that you have a long way to go, so use your Provisions wisely!

Don't forget that your STAMINA score may never exceed its *Initial* value unless specifically instructed on a page. Drinking the Potion of Strength (see later) will restore your STAMINA to its *Initial* level at any time.

Luck

You will find additions to your LUCK score awarded when you have been particularly lucky. Remember that, as with SKILL and STAMINA, your LUCK score may never exceed its *Initial* value unless specifically instructed on a page. Drinking the Potion of Fortune (see later) will restore your LUCK to its *Initial* level at any time, and increase your *Initial* LUCK by 1 point.

EQUIPMENT AND POTIONS

You start your adventure with a sword, leather armour, a shield and a backpack containing Provisions for the trip. But you will find lots more items as the adventure unfolds.

You may also take a magical potion which will aid you on your quest. Each bottle of potion contains enough for *one* measure, i.e. it can only be used **once** during an adventure. Choose ONE of the following:

A Potion of Skill – restores SKILL points.

A Potion of Strength – restores STAMINA points.

A Potion of Fortune – restores LUCK points and adds 1 to *Initial* LUCK.

These potions may be taken at any time during the adventure. Taking a measure of potion will restore SKILL, STAMINA or LUCK scores to their *Initial* level. The Potion of Fortune will increase your *Initial* LUCK score by 1 point and restore LUCK to this new *Initial* level.

HINTS ON PLAY

There is only one true way through the City of Thieves and it will probably take you several attempts to find it. Make notes and draw a map as you explore – this map will be useful in future adventures and help you to identify unexplored sections of the dungeon.

Not all areas contain treasure; many merely contain traps and creatures which you will no doubt fall foul of. There are many 'wild-goose chase' passages and while you may indeed progress through to your ultimate destination, it is by no means certain that you will find what you are searching for.

The 'one true way' involves a minimum of risk and any player, no matter how weak on initial dice rolls, should be able to get through fairly easily.

May the luck of the gods go with you on the adventure ahead!

ALTERNATIVE DICE

If you do not have a pair of dice handy, dice rolls are printed throughout the book at the bottom of the pages. Flicking rapidly through the book and stopping on a page will give you a random dice roll. If you need to 'roll' only one die, read only the first printed die; if two, total the two dice symbols.

FIGHTING FANTASY ADVENTURE SHEET

SKILL
Initial Skill =

STAMINA
Initial Stamina =

LUCK
Initial Luck =

ITEMS OF EQUIPMENT CARRIED

GOLD

JEWELS

POTIONS

PROVISIONS REMAINING

Adventurer's Name ....

MONSTER ENCOUNTER BOXES

SKILL =
STAMINA =

SKILL =
STAMINA =

SKILL =
STAMINA =

SKILL =
STAMINA =

SKILL =
STAMINA =

SKILL =
STAMINA =

SKILL =
STAMINA =

SKILL =
STAMINA =

SKILL =
STAMINA =

TURN OVER IF YOU DARE

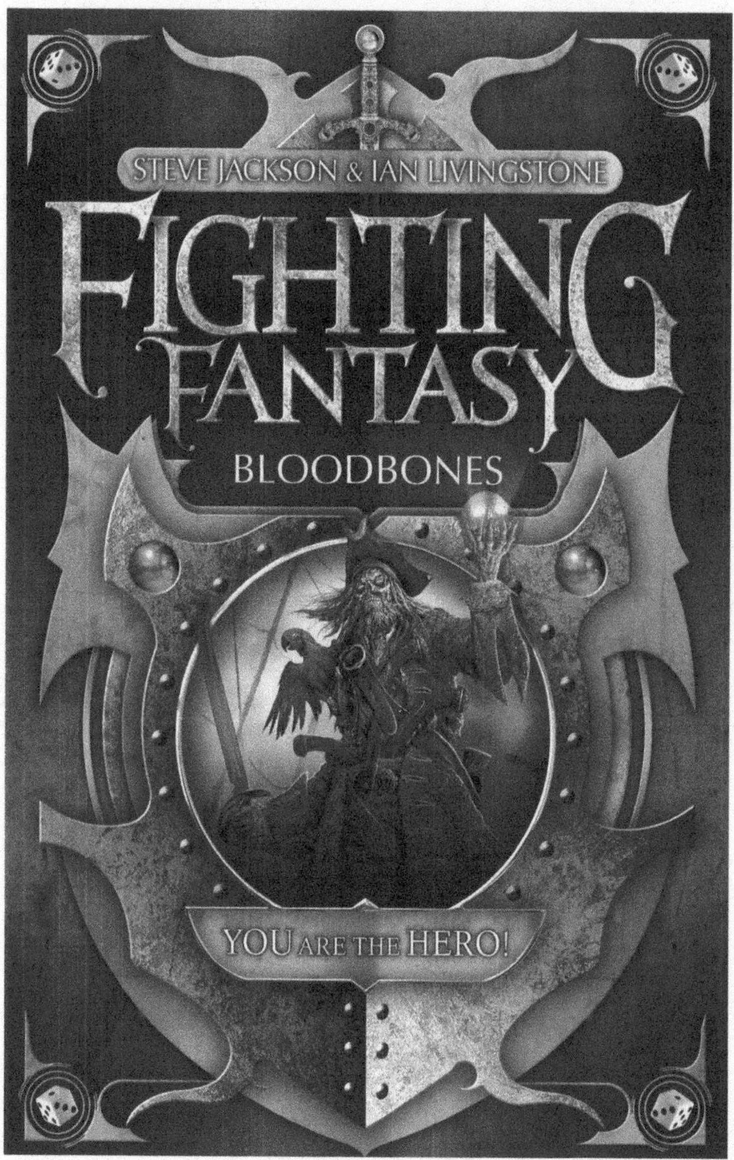

EXCLUSIVE EXTRACT FROM

BLOODBONES

A dreaded pirate-lord.
Dark voodoo magic.
Do YOU have the courage to overcome this scourge of the seas?

It all started ten years ago when the evil pirate-lord Cinnabar murdered your family. For the last six years you have sailed the high seas, searching for a sign of Cinnabar so that you might have your revenge. Recently you heard tell that Cinnabar's galleon, the *Virago*, is frequently seen sailing the waters around Nankunu Bay and that he has a hidden base somewhere close to the Port of Crabs.

Eager to hunt down the villainous pirate, you manage to secure passage on a merchant ship sailing to the Port of Crabs. The town's notoriety precedes it and you know that you are heading towards a despicable place, haven to every pirate, buccaneer and freebooter plying their trade off the coast of the kingdom of Ruddlestone in the Old World.

Upon arriving in the port, you head for the infamous pirate inn, the Jolly Roger. This seems as good a place as any to begin your search and indeed the inn is packed with all manner of scurvy-looking sailors and other lowlifes. Engaging the landlord in conversation you soon move to the topic of Cinnabar. 'I hear the *Virago* plies these waters,' you say. 'I'm surprised we weren't attacked ourselves.'

'Not any more it doesn't,' the landlord replies. 'Have you not heard? Cinnabar has been dead these last six months.'

Cinnabar dead? You have come all this way harbouring desires for revenge, only to find that the dread pirate-lord has already passed from his world!

Disheartened that you were not the one to do away with the evil Cinnabar, you head despondently for the door. You are about to leave the Jolly Roger and head for home when an old man pulls on your arm and mutters, 'Just because he's dead doesn't mean he's at rest. Cinnabar isn't *really* dead see, and he's coming back!' Intrigued at what he has just told you, you agree to meet the old man outside in ten minutes to learn more about Cinnabar's rumoured 'death'.

When the ten minutes are up, you return to the Jolly Roger and sneak down the side alley next to it. But in the misty passage you quickly realise that you are not alone! Three pirates are waiting for you, ugly, scarred rogues, the biggest of which looks as if he has some Ogre blood in his lineage. At the pirates' feet lies the old man, beaten, bruised and only just conscious.

'Here's the snooper', growls the Half Ogre. 'You're no match for us'. The other two pirates burst into coarse laughter, 'Yeah, you're fishbait!'

Turn to paragraph **1**.

1

Still laughing, the ruffians advance towards you. Apart from the Half-Ogre, there is a well-built bearded man, missing most of his teeth and a leaner rouge with two ugly red scars running down the right-hand side of his face. Will you:

Charge one of the pirates? Turn to 7
Stand firm and prepare to fight the rogue? Turn to 4

2

To try to avoid unwanted attention and in order to remain as inconspicuous as possible, you decide to wait until nightfall before investigating potential locations for the pirates' base. Where will you begin your search, in the taverns and inns of the city (turn to **10**) or around the docks (turn to **5**)?

3

The Half-Ogre moves in to attack you with his club.

HALF-OGRE	SKILL 8	STAMINA 9

If the Half-Ogre wins the Attack Round, roll one dice. On a roll of 6, the blow from his club knocks you off your feet. This means that you spend the next round of combat getting up again, so you must reduce your Attack Strength by 2 points for that Attack Round. If you kill the Half-Ogre, turn to **6**.

4

Swinging their cudgels, the pirates engage you in combat.

	SKILL	STAMINA
First PIRATE	7	7
Second PIRATE	6	7

If you win, the Half-Ogre steps forward to fight you. Will you face your opponent (turn to **3**) or try to escape (turn to **8**)?

5

The docks are quiet at this time of night. You decide that if the pirates' hideout was located around the docks, the entrance would have to be in the harbour wall somewhere. Descending to the wooden jetties, you start your search. *Thud.* What was that? *Thud.* There it is again. You stand perfectly still, your ears straining to pick up any sound. Then you hear the rattling of a chain being dragged across the wooden planks close by. *Swoosh!* A large anchor suddenly flies out of the dense mist, in a sweeping arc towards you …

To discover what danger larks within the shadows, you will have to continue the adventure in **Bloodbones.** ***Can you end Cinnabar's reign of terror by destroying the pirate captain and his crew of cutthroats once and once all?***
Come hell or high water Bloodbones must be stopped!

6

The last of the pirates falls and with some relief you sheathe your sword. It looks as if the pirates have beaten the old man within an inch of his life and he is failing fast. You do your best to make the old man comfortable and he opens his eyes. 'Thanks stranger,' he gasps, 'but I'm a goner now. They're up to something you know.' You ask him who he's talking about. 'Cinnabar's crew, the Pirates of the Black Skull.' Looking at the hands of the old man's assailants, you see that each bears the tattoo of a grinning black skull. 'I've seen them meeting up again around the taverns in the city; Silas Gallows, Keelhaul Jack, old Crivens, even Malu the Witchdoctor. They're planning something all right. Rumour says Mirel the Red found Cinnabar's body and that he's not rightly dead. But he's not rightly alive either, see. It's all that Voodoo and black magic they meddle in. Not right so it isn't'. He coughs weakly: 'He's coming back. We'll all be doomed! Stranger, beware the Black Skull, Bloodbones is coming back!' And then he is gone. Laying the old man down, you ponder his last words and what your next action should be.

So Cinnabar is not really dead. In that case you may still be revenged. But what did the old man mean when he said that Cinnabar is not really alive either? You have been given several clues about your enemy and where you should start your search for him. The old man mentioned that the Pirates of the Black Skull were gathering again in the Port of Crabs so they may have a hidden base somewhere in the city, but of course at present you have no idea where it may be.

You could now visit some of the taverns and inns yourself, in the hope of finding out more (turn to **10**) or you could abandon your search for further information and instead look for the pirates' hidden base (turn to **2**).

7

The pirates are not expecting this reaction from you and you are able to wound one of the rogues before they know what is going on. Fight them both at the same time.

	SKILL	STAMINA
First PIRATE	6	5
Second PIRATE	6	7

If you win, the Half-Ogre steps forward to fight you. Turn to **3** to fight him or to escape turn to **8**.

8

Taking flight, you hear a sharp crack behind you and then find yourself falling forwards as the Half-Ogre's whip wraps around your ankles and your feet are pulled from beneath you. Lose 2 Stamina points. Dropping his whip, the Half-Ogre moves in to attack you with his club.

HALF-OGRE	SKILL 8	STAMINA 9

If the Half-Ogre wins an Attack Round, roll one die. On a roll of 6, the blow from his club knocks you off your feet. This means that you spend the next round of combat getting up again, so you must reduce your Attack Strength by 2 points for that Attack Round. If you kill the Half-Ogre, turn to **6**.

9

Running hell-for-leather, you round a corner and run straight into more of Cinnabar's pirates. You are soon overcome. Receiving a blow to the back of your head from a heavy cosh, you lose consciousness …

What will happen to you now that you are in the pirates' grasp? Is there any way out? Only the bravest warrior can battle the dark powers of voodoo and put an end to Cinnabar's evil once and for all. Take up the challenge and continue your adventure in **Bloodbones*!***

10

You visit many of the seediest drinking establishments in the city, including The Cat and Cockroach, Angar's Mutiny and the Barnacle Tavern. However your enquires and investigations attract the attentions of those whose interest you did not want to arouse. Having just left yet another smoky bar-room, you suddenly find yourself confronted by a group of pirates and black-robed devotees – all followers of Quezkari. They have been alerted to your mission by your endless enquiries. Realising the danger you are in from Cinnabar's cronies, you run for it, as there are far too many for you to fight by yourself. *Test your Luck*. If you are Lucky, you escape to the docks (turn to **5**). If you are Unlucky turn to **9**.

ONLINE

Stay in touch with the Fighting Fantasy community at www.fightingfantasy.com. Sign up today and receive exclusive access to:

- Fresh Adventure Sheets
- Members' forum
- Competitions
- Quizzes and polls
- Exclusive Fighting Fantasy news and updates

You can also send in your own Fighting Fantasy material, the very best of which will make it onto the website.

www.fightingfantasy.com

The website where YOU ARE THE HERO!